"I thought we might dance."

Her eyes widened. "Dance?"

Mitch fought a surge of frustration at her obvious dismay. Hiding his annoyance, he smiled instead, allowing just a touch of cynicism to show.

He slipped an arm around her waist and lifted his free hand. "You hold this one."

Elaine swallowed visibly. "I'd rather not."

"It's a dance, Elaine," he grumbled, taking her hand and lacing their fingers together. "Part of the deal was that you and I act like friends."

Renee Roszel has been writing romance novels since 1983 and simply loves her job. She likes to keep her stories humorous and light, with her heroes gorgeous, sexy and larger than life. She says, "Why not spend your days and nights with the very best?" Luckily for Renee, her husband is gorgeous and sexy, too!

Renee loves to hear from her readers. Send your letter and SASE to: P.O. Box 700154, Tulsa, Oklahoma 74170. Or visit her Web site at: www.ReneeRoszel.com

Books by Renee Roszel

HARLEQUIN ROMANCE®
3599—HONEYMOON HITCH*
3603—COMING HOME TO WED*
3644—ACCIDENTAL FIANCÉE*
3660—TO CATCH A BRIDE
3682—HER HIRED HUSBAND

*The Merits of Marriage

THE TYCOON'S TEMPTATION
Renee Roszel

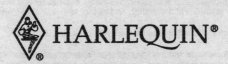

HARLEQUIN®

TORONTO • NEW YORK • LONDON
AMSTERDAM • PARIS • SYDNEY • HAMBURG
STOCKHOLM • ATHENS • TOKYO • MILAN • MADRID
PRAGUE • WARSAW • BUDAPEST • AUCKLAND

To TDW3
Wherever you may roam
Be like E.T.
Phone home

ISBN 0-373-03705-8

THE TYCOON'S TEMPTATION

First North American Publication 2002.

CHAPTER ONE

A HEARTLESS, faceless robber baron was stealing Elaine's home, and there was nothing on earth she could do to stop it. Jarred from her angry thoughts by a tap on her shoulder, she flicked off the vacuum sweeper and turned around. "Yes, Aunt Claire?"

The older woman wiped her hands on her jeans and blew a salt-and-pepper curl back up to join the kinky corona that stood out from her head. "Supper time, Lainey. Take a break. You've been working like a Trojan since five this morning." When Elaine started to protest, her aunt held up a halting hand. "We've got two more weeks before you have to move out of this big old mausoleum. You don't need to kill yourself trying to clean it all today."

She pulled a checkered bandanna from the pocket of her red flannel shirt and rubbed at Elaine's cheek in her big-sisterly way. "How did you get soot on your face just vacuuming?"

Elaine tried to smile at her aunt's attempt at humor, but her effort failed miserably. She knew the woman who raised her was trying to lift her spirits with teasing banter. As if readying this historic mansion to be handed over to a ruthless pirate were no more unpalatable than a stroll in the park.

Unfortunately, considering Elaine's awful situation, the biggest genius in the comedy business, doing his most brilliant shtick, wouldn't get her to crack a smile these days. She was going bankrupt, losing her busi-

5

ness and all her savings, plus every penny her aunt could scrape together. This estate had been in her husband's family for generations, and she'd lost that, too. Not to mention the tragedy of her husband's death—and the guilt that nagged her, no matter how irrational. No one in her right mind could find a reason to smile.

She swallowed hard, struggling to dislodge the lump of sadness that seemed to permanently reside in her throat. She released her death grip on the vacuum and pushed a stray wisp of her hair under the green scarf she'd wrapped around her head. "I cleaned out the master suite's fireplace."

"With your face?" Her aunt wet the bandanna with a little spit and aimed for Elaine's nose, but she ducked out of reach. "Hold still, Lainey."

"Please, Aunt Claire." Elaine rubbed the back of her wrist across her nose, fearing she was making it worse. Still, at twenty-seven she was decades too old to have her face swabbed like that. Wiping her hands on her faded jeans, she sighed long and low. Bone-weary, she had neither the strength nor will to argue. Besides, she supposed she should eat, since she couldn't recall having a bite all day. Indicating the back of the house, she said, "Okay, let's go make some sandwiches."

The booming impact of the door's heavy, brass knocker echoed like cannon fire in the foyer, ricocheting off the high walls and lofty ceiling of the living room where Elaine and her aunt stood. "Oh, that's little Harry with my toothpaste and shoe laces."

The older woman indicated her scuffed hiking boots with a wave. "These old things've been broken and knotted so many times I can't lace 'em past my instep." Claire waved toward the entry hall, with its scenic wallpaper and generously bunched curtains, all the more opulent with the overlong, purple velvet fabric laying in swathes on the parquet floor. The French, nineteenth-century crystal chandelier sparkled in the late-afternoon sunshine, throwing off rainbows of vivid color, making the place seem like a fantasy castle in the clouds.

Elaine's breath caught as her gaze drifted across the space, an exotic mix of baroque and rococo. Even after living there a year, every room continued to be an awe-inspiring feast for the eye. With its gilt and inlaid furnishings, hand-painted walls, Aubusson carpets and festooning drapery, the Stuben family home was a rich, eclectic masterpiece.

And now she had lost it to her creditors. For the millionth time a stab of guilt cut deep, making her cringe.

"You get the door, Lainey," her aunt said as she turned toward the exit to the kitchen. "I'll start supper."

Elaine felt her aunt's urging push. "And pay Harry the fifty cents I promised him for running those things over here for me. He's saving up for a new bicycle. That clap-trappy piece of junk he rides is a hazard."

Elaine headed for the foyer. "That twelve-year-old kid will be able to buy a new bike before I can pay for new shoes," she murmured to herself. Though she could hardly afford it, she didn't want to ask her aunt for the fifty cents. Thanks to her, Claire's finances were suffering, too.

Besides, Harry was a great kid. He worked hard at his after-school job. He deserved a safe bicycle.

She pictured freckle-faced Harry Browne in her mind. The heart-tugging, chipped front tooth that showed itself when he grinned. The hole in the knee of oversize jeans, and the backward Chicago Cubs ball cap planted over scraggly red hair. All in all, Harry was a sweet wad of little-boy perfection. She'd agonized over having to lay off his single mom from her job on the kitchen staff. At least she'd managed to find JoBeth Browne work at the nearby supermarket.

Focusing her attention on dislodging two quarters from a hip pocket, Elaine tugged open the mammoth cherrywood door. She extracted the change from her jeans—two quarters and a linty, gray button. The plastic button didn't look familiar, and from the lint clinging to it, she had a feeling it hadn't been missed from wherever it belonged. Shoving it back in her hip pocket, she said, "Here you go, sweetie-pie. Thanks for..." She held out the money, looked up, her sentence dying a quick death.

Instead of the twelve-year-old, chipped-toothed moppet she expected to see, a much larger figure loomed on the stone porch. At the moment she found herself staring in the vicinity of a man's chest. A surge of feminine awareness coursed through her and she instinctively moved back a step, sensing something—or someone—out of the ordinary.

Backlit by a pale winter sun on the verge of setting, the towering stranger was clad in a black cashmere trench coat. Impressively built, his six-and-a-half-foot frame almost filled the stone archway. Though Elaine was five-eight, and far from anorexic, she seemed to shrink by half, and felt peculiarly fragile.

Though her glimpse had been a paltry second or two, she felt something she couldn't quite put a name to. It was the sort of awe one might get when gazing at a mighty fortress—unconquerable mortar and stone.

What an odd thought to have about a flesh-and-blood person! She shook herself and focused on the man's face.

His eyes drew her first, the deep blue of a clear night sky. Heavy-lidded with thick, ebony lashes, they held a striking allure that stirred something deep inside her. At first glance they seemed like two pools of boundless darkness, yet as she stared, she sensed more than saw, a hint of heat in their depths. It was like being conscious of a faraway cabin with a welcoming fire. Yet at the same time being filled with fear that the warm haven might be too distant to be reached before succumbing to the wintry chill. That unmistakable reserve, that "stand back" quality, intimidated her. She swallowed, startled to notice her throat had gone bone-dry.

Those deceptively sleepy eyelids slid down slightly, narrowing his gaze. Well-formed lips curved in a wry grin for a couple of heartbeats before he dropped his gaze. Lifting hands swathed in supple, black leather, he began to remove his gloves, tugging one finger at a time. She watched the slow, deliberate movements in some kind of weird trance.

Once he'd removed the gloves, he placed them together, folded them fingers-over-palm, then deposited them in his overcoat pocket. When he finally resumed eye contact, he lifted a hand. "You're welcome," he said, pinching the silver she held between his fingers. With hardly any effort he extracted the coins and tossed them in the air. They glittered for an instant before landing with a light ka-chink in the center of his palm. "People rarely meet me at the door with money *and* endearments." He pocketed the change.

His pleasant baritone registered more on Elaine's spine than in her consciousness. A tingle frolicked up and down her back at the throaty sound. But the words were jumbled, making little sense. Obviously her mind wasn't functioning up to par. She blinked several times in an attempt to jump-start her brain cells.

After a third and forth blink, one thing managed to get through. He was making fun of her. The next fact that registered was that he'd actually *taken* fifty cents she couldn't afford to toss away.

Her momentary mental lapse ended and she experienced a wave of annoyance, giving him a critical once-over. Besides the expensive coat, he wore a high-priced, black suit and polished, hand-sewn wingtips. Her late husband had worn hand-sewn shoes, too, so she knew something about quality men's wear. That maroon and gold tie he sported cost five hundred dollars if it cost a dime.

Even though this stranger's expression had lost even the brief semblance of a grin, his hawkish features were elegant and arresting. His hair, the color of a raven's wing, was scrupulously trimmed. He was the epitome of an upper-echelon executive. Maybe he was an old Harvard chum of her late husband's. But if he'd come to pay his last respects he was late by nearly half a year.

As Elaine scanned his face, she sensed he did not give away smiles freely, but when he did, it would be quite a sight. Though the Chicago temperature on that January day was well below freezing, and several inches of white lingered on the lawn from the last snowfall, that thought about his smile sent an unruly heat racing through her, a heat that started in her belly and spread outward.

She gulped in a breath of frigid air, confused about where all this unwarranted feminine appreciation was coming from. Grappling for composure, she cleared her throat. "Um—may I help you?"

He arched a brow as though that should be obvious. "I'm here to see the mistress of the house."

She was a little insulted that he assumed she was the help. If the truth were told, Elaine had been forced to discharge the household staff months ago. Sneaking a peek at herself, in jeans, sneakers and the dull brown turtleneck sweater, she faced the fact she didn't look much like the mistress of a stately mansion.

She straightened her shoulders. "Please, state your business."

He watched her for a moment before replying, "I'd be happy to." After a pause, he added, "To the mistress of the house."

Elaine was annoyed by the man's impertinence. Well, he could go jump for all she cared. "Then you can't see her. Mrs. Stuben is a busy woman." She surprised herself, being so brusque. Not to mention she was lying. After all, he was "seeing" the mistress of the mansion right now. At least she'd be its mistress for fourteen more days.

Maybe it was this past, horrible year since her ill-conceived marriage. Guy's sudden change from doting and sensitive suitor before the wedding, then on the honeymoon witnessing his shocking metamorphosis. Before her eyes he'd become a domineering, controlling brute with a sick need to have his ego constantly stroked. Not to mention his jealous rages every time she spoke to another man.

Then his sudden, tragic death five months ago. And after that, her day-and-night battle to save her Internet business. Maybe all of that together had made up the ingredients for the mortar that had given her this

go-to-Hades grit. Or maybe she was simply so exhausted, so world-weary, she didn't have the capacity
to guard her tongue any longer.

Whatever it was, her outburst caused Mr. Tall, Dark
and Trouble to lift an eyebrow at her. That was the
second eyebrow lift in as many minutes! "Look, it's
cold," she said less snappishly. "State your business
or move along."

He crossed his arms, the pause an eloquent warning.
"Please tell the busy Mrs. Stuben, Mitchell Rath would
appreciate an audience."

"Mitchell Ra..." She'd almost repeated his entire
name before she realized saying it aloud would not
make the news any more palatable. "You—you're
Mitchell Rath?"

He nodded, then held out a hand as though he expected her to take it. "And you're the very busy Mrs.
Stuben."

He surprised her by referring to her by her name.
Resentment heated her cheeks. He hadn't been taken
in by her huffy impersonation of a domestic. "What—
what—how do you know I'm Mrs. Stuben?" She refused to take his hand—*the hand of the robber baron
who was picking the bones of her company, buying her
out for pennies on the dollar and stealing her home!*

His gaze roved casually up to the cotton scarf cov-
ering her hair, then slid slowly, deliberately, downward
to settle on her scuffed and dingy sneakers. After pon-
derous seconds, the critical excursion apparently complete, his eyes once again met hers. "How do I know
you're Mrs. Stuben?" His lips drooped sensuously at
the corners in a facial shrug. "You can't be the help,"
he drawled. "They dress better."

He gave her enough time to grasp his taunt but not

enough to respond before he reached out, barely touching the tip of her nose. She caught a whiff of a woodsy aftershave. "What is that on your face?"

The soot! She'd forgotten about the dratted soot!

She cringed. Not only was this man profiting from her financial ruin, he found it necessary to ridicule her, too! Furious and too tired to watch her mouth, she said, "It's vulture repellent! *Obviously* I sh-should have used more!"

She stared him down, her eyes telegraphing the question, *How do you like being ridiculed?*

He blinked, but Elaine couldn't tell if a wince had been involved or not. "You're shivering, Mrs. Stuben." He indicated the foyer. "Why don't we move our mutual admiration society meeting inside before you catch pneumonia?"

A rattling, clanking noise caught Elaine's attention. She spotted Harry peddling down the long, snow-cleared curricular drive. Her unwelcome companion turned as the twelve-year-old pumped his skinny legs, steering the bike around the sporty silver Mercedes parked at the bottom of the flagstone stairs.

Harry hopped off his bike on the run and scampered up the half-dozen steps, shucking his backpack as he came. "Miz Elaine, here's Miz Claire's package." He sounded a little winded, and his breath frosted the air. Showing off his chipped-tooth grin, he held out the crumpled brown sack he'd extracted from his pack. His attention skittered to the tall man. "Hi," he said, oblivious to the fact that he was speaking to the notorious "Vulture," renowned for swooping in on dying Internet businesses, buying up the carcasses and selling off the bones for personal gain. He'd made himself a wealthy man dismembering the remains of such broken businesses. And now he was dismembering hers.

"Hello," Mitchell Rath said, startling Elaine out of her furious musings. She shot him a look, surprised to see him grin at the boy. Even in profile, she experienced a feminine flutter at that glitter of white teeth. She hurriedly shifted her gaze to Harry. "Hi, Mr. Browne," she said with as much enthusiasm as her gloomy mood would allow. "Want to come in for cocoa?"

He shook his head, repositioning the red and blue Cubs cap. "Gotta get back to help Mom at the store. Mr. Goff said he'd give me two whole dollars if I'd sweep out the back room and break down some boxes."

"Two dollars, huh?" Elaine managed a smile. Henry was such a super kid she couldn't help herself. "I'd better let you get going, then." She reached in her pocket, then remembered who'd snatched Harry's fifty cents. She cast her tall nemesis a frown. "*You* have his money." She had to bite her tongue to keep from adding, *"Of course, pocketing other people's cash is what you do!"*

She sensed he got her message, by the slight narrowing of his eyes. Reaching into his coat pocket, he pulled out several bills and handed them to the boy.

Harry fingered the bills and Elaine thought she saw a five among them. There had to be at least eight dollars there.

"*Holy cow! Thanks,* mister!" Harry's grin grew broad. Aiming a hand toward the sports car, he asked, "Those your wheels?"

The man in black nodded. "It's a rental."

Harry's wolf whistle astonished Elaine. She'd never

heard him whistle with such heartfelt, grown-up gusto. "Someday I'm gonna *own* me cool wheels like that, dude."

The tall man chuckled, the sound deep and rich in the cold, gray stillness. "I imagine you will."

The man's light compliment seemed to mean a great deal to Harry, for his eyes went wide and his grin grew broader. "You really think so?"

"Absolutely." The man winked. "I'm never wrong."

"Gee-thanks!" Turning back for a quick wave, he added, "Miz Elaine, call Mom at the store if you need anything tomorrow. See ya." He faced Mitchell Rath again, and paused. "See ya?" The question was almost a plea.

"You bet."

Elaine flicked the man a frown, irked at him for leading the boy on that way. It wasn't as though Harry hadn't already had a father abandon him. Did he really need men like Mitchell Rath making him careless, absurd promises? Arranging her expression to feign light-heartedness, she waved at Harry. "*I'll* see you tomorrow—for sure!"

"'kay!" He grabbed up his bike and clanked away.

"Well?" came a deep voice, too close for comfort.

She jerked to glare at her offensive caller. With the remnants of a smile lingering on his lips he was pulse-poundingly handsome. Furious with her hormones for their demented betrayal, she glowered at him. "Well, *what?*"

"Do we go inside?" He eyed her, his expression challenging. "For the record, Mrs. Stuben, it *is* my house."

She bristled. "Not for two weeks!"

His jaw worked and Elaine had the distinct impression he was disturbed. She experienced a swell of gratitude. Good! For once she was upsetting him! When he shrugged out of his coat and moved toward her, she lurched a step backward. "What are you doing?"

Undaunted by her suspicious recoil, he slung his coat over her shoulders. The voluminous cashmere engulfed her all the way to her ankles. She was shocked by how toasty warm it was, almost like being cloaked in an electric blanket, yet its warmth was all male animal, all his. The same, woodsy scent floated around her, uninvited yet irresistibly pleasant, capturing her senses.

"If you intend to stand out here debating the issue for the whole two weeks, you'll need a coat."

"I only intend to stand here debating as long as you're here!"

"Try two weeks."

"Two—t-two…" Her voice faltered and died. This time her stutter wasn't due to the winter chill, but to the suggestion that he would be in Chicago for two weeks. It was the worst possible melodrama she could dream up—even in her most horrifying nightmare. She couldn't have heard right. "You—you're *not* staying?" she demanded in disbelief.

He pursed his lips. Apparently his lack of response was supposed to be all the answer she needed.

Elaine feared she had lost her mind to frostbite. The coat had come too late to save her gray matter. Why on earth would he threaten her this way? How could this happen? Why was he here two weeks early? Was it possible he planned to steal even her final few days in this place that had been her home for the past year? There was so much to do. Packing and cleaning and—

and besides, she hadn't found another job or place to live.

He stared at her for a slow count of three, then shook his head as though her bullheadedness was beyond belief. Grasping her arm, he hauled her into the foyer. "Why, thank you, a tour of the house would be very nice."

The door boomed shut as Mr. Rath took it upon himself to move them both inside. She jerked from his grasp and spun on him. "Never put your hands on me! I've had all the controlling I can take for one..." *No, Elaine! You will not blurt out your personal problems to this man!* Another voice in her head tried to say something about how doting and attentive Guy had been when they'd met. With the distinction of an Ivy League MBA, a first-class family pedigree and the believable veneer of charm, he'd been impossible to say no to. Not to the whirlwind courtship or the marriage. After that it had been too late.

Guy's unreasoning jealousy and bullying temperament had been a shock. Mere days after the wedding she wasn't allowed to make a move without Guy's permission. And her associations with male clients in her e-business had sent him into fits of rage.

He'd charged into her textile art e-business with big ideas for expansion. Fearful of his explosive temper, she hadn't known how to extricate herself from his tyranny. He essentially took over what Elaine had been slowly and steadily building for five years. What had begun as a small outlet for handmade quilts was evolving into a respected market for the discriminating customer in search of custom textile art.

Guy's petty jealousies and tin-god attitude coupled with his billowing ego turned out to be calamitous for

Elaine's marriage as well as her business. He'd scorned her worries, dived in headfirst pitching marketing schemes, negotiating contracts, making promises she and her crew of talented seamstresses could not physically meet.

"For one—what?"

The question yanked her from her dark musings and she started, refocusing her anger in a more appropriate direction. Toward the man who'd plundered her business. She mustn't be angry at the dead. Though on the very day Guy died, she'd finally found the courage to walk out. Their seven-month marriage and business partnership had been a nightmare. She'd already packed a bag and had planned to tell him it was over that night. Instead, the tragic news of his death had come. From that day until this, she hadn't been able to shed the irrational belief her desire to get out of a bad marriage had somehow sealed his fate.

She swallowed over a lump in her throat. With Guy Stuben dead, the clout of his family name was gone. Almost before Elaine could take a breath, the loan was called. The last five months had been worse than five years in Hades as she'd struggled to live up to the merciless contract Guy had pledged them to. Floundering in overwhelming debt and working under impossible conditions, she'd fought with every fiber of her being to save her company.

She exhaled long and low. All that was in the past now. The business was gone. All her money, gone. Claire's too. The physical bits and pieces of her company belonged to Mitchell Rath, including this estate. She needed to face that and come to terms with it. She needed to begin to work through her feelings of guilt. Start over, get a job, save enough to begin her textile art e-business again. *On her own terms this time. No more stupid, rash decisions about men, either!*

"You've had all the controlling for one—what," he repeated slowly, as though he already knew but insisted that she say it out loud.

Not likely, Mr. Rath! You may have picked the bones of my business carcass but you aren't going to feast on my personal life! She glared at him. "*Nothing.* Forget it," she said. "What do you care?"

His gaze hardened for a split second, but he didn't immediately respond. It was almost as though she'd hurt his feelings. *Ha! That was a laugh. What feelings?*

His gaze probed for a moment before he shrugged and let his attention drift away to scan the elegant foyer. "Forgive me. I didn't mean to pry." His voice was full and rich, very pleasant to listen to. Elaine sensed it was the sort of voice that made women turn and search a room to discover its source. "I'll take that, if you're through with it," he said.

She was confused and frowned.

He inclined his head toward her. "My coat."

Feeling stupid for letting herself get sidetracked by anything so frivolously superficial as a voice, she shrugged off the overcoat, shoving it at him.

"Thank you," he said. "Now, if you'll show me to my room?"

She stared, dumbfounded. After a few thundering heartbeats she found the ability to speak. "*Your* room?" How dare he assume she would let him stay! His company lawyers had promised her she had two more weeks of ownership before he was to take possession. It hadn't been in writing, but she'd assumed the man would keep his word! "Try the Holiday Inn."

"Or—the master suite?" He glanced around, seem-

ingly looking for something. "That would be traditional."

"Tr-tra…" She was speechless. "That's my room."

He walked away from her, toward the foyer closet.
After he'd hung up his coat, he turned, his dark eyes
mesmerizing. Elaine refused to be affected, telling herself the glittering hue was perfect for the cold, heartless
creature that he was. And she'd thought she'd seen
warmth in their depths! *Double ha!*

His head dipped in a nod. "Since the master suite is
taken, something with a southern exposure, then?" His
behavior was oddly suggestive of a chivalrous enemy
granting a small concession.

"'Southern exposure?'" she echoed, highly dubious. "I'd think you'd want the coldest room in the
house—to keep the ice water in your veins sufficiently
chilled!"

The room held a deathly hush. His gaze grasped hers
and held. His eyes sparked with indignant anger, with
just a touch of Mount Olympus aloofness to let her
know he would not strike out. That steely gaze com-
bined with the eerie sensuality he radiated was getting
under her skin. She didn't like the torrid effect it had
on her. *He was the dreaded Vulture, for heaven's sake!*

"I realize this is an imposition, Mrs. Stuben." His
voice shattering the stillness, made her jump. "I'll try
not to cause you any undue stress."

She regained her poise with difficulty, disconcerted
and angry with herself for allowing this heartless an-
droid to affect her in any way but with utter loathing.
"You can't be serious."

"About not wanting to cause you stress?"

She choked out a derisive laugh. "Oh sure! That'll
happen. No, not about your oh-so-fake desire not to

cause me *undue* stress, about suggesting *I* would consider staying under the same roof with you!'' She shook her head vehemently. ''Not *one* night, sir!'' She lifted her chin, grim as death. ''Let alone *two* whole weeks!''

He slipped his hands into his trouser pockets, looking princely even as his nostrils flared with offense. ''Of course, it's your decision.''

His seeming ease at her threat to walk out made her see red. ''You have no compunctions about throwing people out of their homes?''

He slanted her a look that seemed to say, ''Whose home?''

''Well, according to the agreement, I'm supposed to be able to stay here for two more weeks!''

''I didn't ask you to leave, Mrs. Stuben.''

That was true enough. Flustered and furious, she crossed her arms and pointedly looked away. A quick, disturbing thought struck like a two-by-four to the back of the head, and she gasped. ''So *that's* your game?'' She aimed an accusing finger at his chest. ''You won't *make* me leave, but you know I won't stay.'' She moved a step toward him, itching to slap his handsome face. ''Brilliant strategy! You can take away a person's home *weeks* early, and without violating any contracts, because you're too detestable to be around!''

Though he didn't immediately respond to her savaging, she detected a definite deepening of his tan.

He watched her for a long, tense moment, his expression closed. The only sign that he wasn't a statue was the occasional flare of his nostrils.

With the drawn-out assault of his narrowed gaze, Elaine began to tremble.

''Well, then, Mrs. Stuben,'' he said at last, his voice low and controlled. ''Don't let me keep you.''

CHAPTER TWO

THE woman who'd met Mitch at the door gaped at him, clearly not expecting his quiet invitation that she leave. Mitch was a little surprised, himself, since that wasn't what he wanted. His whole plan, his reason for being there, depended on Elaine Stuben. She couldn't move out. He wouldn't allow it.

Those wide, green eyes blinked several times. He sensed she was struggling to hold back tears and cursed inwardly. He hated this. He hated being here. He was accustomed to cutting a check and having his lawyers deal with the human side of these transactions.

Long ago he'd insulated himself from the world's wretched and disenfranchised, disciplined his emotions to resist the pull of liquid-eyed pleas. It was a lesson his parents taught him all too thoroughly throughout his formative years, sharing their meager, open-handed existence and witnessing their unapologetic mistakes. Since Mitchell inherited his parents genes, he knew he was genetically predisposed to be a sucker, a chump, a pushover to a sad story, so he'd spent his adult years hardening his heart against pleading and weeping.

Her lower lip began to tremble and he experienced an unwelcome twinge of compassion. Though he refused to act on it, he couldn't extract his gaze from that quivering bit of anatomy. She bit down on it, then whirled away. Annoyed with himself for feeling anything, he watched as she escaped.

She ran from the foyer through a hallway which led

into the bowels of the house. He was confused. He'd thought she would rush to her room to pack. In most mansions, bedrooms would be upstairs somewhere over the grand staircase. And this mansion's staircase was grand, indeed. Massive and gilded, it curved down from a second-floor balcony, spilling regally into the foyer. Its rich, Oriental carpet runner was a striking counterpoint to the gleam of the parquet floor.

Possibly Mrs. Stuben's plan was to run straight out a back door to a car, then disappear into greater Chicago. He decided he'd better follow. His game plan didn't include filing a missing persons report on a headstrong female who plainly would prefer to be devoured by lions than spend one night under the same roof with him.

"Your preference be damned, lady," he muttered, the sharp clip of his heels echoing around him as he strode after her.

It didn't take long to realize she hadn't run out the back. He heard female voices, one distressed. That would be Mrs. Green Eyes. The other female sounded concerned and somewhat older.

"But, Lainey, where will we go? My new floor furnace won't be delivered before February third. That's two weeks away. It's too cold for us to stay there without heat."

"A hotel, then," the younger woman cried.

"What do we pay with?" There was a pause, and Mitch thought he heard a long, mournful sigh. "We lost my money, too, trying to save your..." The sentence dwindled away.

"Oh, Aunt Claire," the younger voice began, "What are we going to do?"

Mitch had heard enough. Eavesdropping hadn't been

on his agenda, but it gave him the ammunition he needed to coerce little Mrs. Not One Night, Sir! into reconsidering an abrupt departure—no matter how detestable the concept might be for her. She had a great deal to gain if she stayed, and nothing to lose—only some face-to-face time with him. No doubt, in her mind, a distressing price to pay. But blast it, being around The Vulture *was* survivable.

He rounded the corner into an industrial-size kitchen with so much shiny stainless steel and white tile he felt as if he might go blind. The only non-white, non-stainless elements in the place were the woman and a couple of plates containing sandwiches and potato chips on the stainless countertop.

All that soot on Mrs. Stuben's face didn't mask the rosy hue of anger in her cheeks. The older woman's complexion was ruddier than Mrs. Stuben's, as though she spent much of her time outside. Her bright flannel shirt and flyaway hair gave her an interesting look, like a woman with zest for life. Mitch liked her immediately, then frowned at the thought. He didn't plan to make *friends* out of these people. They would be useful, for a time. That was all.

The pair must have heard him, or the darkness of his suit against all that brightness caught their peripheral visions, for they turned in unison. Mrs. Stuben glared. The other woman stared, looking disconcerted. He could see the family resemblance in the two. The older woman, Mitch guessed to be around fifty. Maturity had ripened her frame by a few pounds, but she looked like a woman in good physical shape. Her nose was longer and thin enough to slice cheese. But she had the same wide-set, green eyes and generous lips as her niece, and was attractive in a scrubbed, no-nonsense way.

"Take any room in the place," the young Mrs. Stuben ground out. "We'll be gone as soon as we pack."

Mitch succeeded in suppressing his aggravation, but just barely, and summoned a diplomatic facade. "Thank you." This would take finesse. It was one business tactic he had little use for. Desperate people didn't need to be finessed. They knew his offer would be the best of a bad situation. If they were to salvage anything, Mitchell Rath was the man to call. However, the reason he'd come to Chicago *would* require finesse, so he might as well get some practice.

"Don't thank me," she scoffed. "It's your house, remember?"

He nodded. "So it is." Indicating the second woman, he asked, "And who is this—lovely lady?" He graced the older woman with a smile calculated to charm.

The pretty Mrs. Stuben glowered, her lips thin. She didn't look as though she was buying his chivalrous act. She might be a lousy business woman but she was no fool.

After a tense silence, the second woman, said, "I'm Claire Brooke, Elaine's aunt." Her cheeks reddened considerably at his compliment, nearly the same shade as her shirt. Her lips even lifted in a little smile. "I've been staying here with Elaine since she—uh—released the staff. To help get the place ready for—its new owner."

Mitch had a sense about this woman. She was a giver. A do-gooder. Kindness and generosity fairly oozed from her pores. She reminded him of his own mother and he felt the familiar pang of loss. She died when he was twelve, and it still hurt to recall...he cleared his throat, retaining his smile with difficulty. "How do you do, Mrs. Brooke?"

"Miss," she corrected. "I'm one of those old maids or, as a quilter by trade, you might call me a career woman. Whichever label you prefer."

"And I'm The Vulture—or The Magician." He inclined his head in a slight bow. "Whichever label you prefer."

"*Magician?*" Elaine sounded dubious. "Why, because you turn other people's hard-earned money into *yours?*"

The pointed question made him flinch, but he didn't let her see. "No, Mrs. Stuben. Because I turn wreckage into gold."

"That's what I said. Your gold!"

He counted to ten, reining in his temper. "Let's take your company, for instance." He tried to sound politely instructive. "In your inventory, you had seven hundred identical fabric wall-hangings with a bank logo worked into the design. You couldn't complete the remaining order on time, so the bank canceled on you and went elsewhere. Now you have seven hundred useless, worthless wall hangings."

"It was textile art. Handmade, textile art," she said stiffly.

"Whatever." He waved away her argument. "I found a chain of discount stores willing to buy them, cut them up and make throw pillows out of them. Suddenly they're no longer worthless." He shrugged, slipping his hands into his pockets. "Gold."

She swallowed, but her glare raged on. Her fiery cheeks and nose, smudged all over with soot, had a peculiar affect on him. He found himself wondering how she might look with a clean face, her hair out from under that rag. Airy wisps of the stuff fluttered here and there. Curly, glinting golden-red in the fluorescent lighting. It looked clean and soft. He pondered how it would feel—

With a start, he realized where his mind had drifted and mentally shook himself. *What the hell is with you, Rath?*

"I repeat," she muttered. "*Your* gold."

"Not entirely." He forced his thoughts to businesses and away from her hair. "I paid you a fair price."

She eyed heaven.

"And you were happy to get it," he added, holding on to his civil tone with difficulty.

She scowled but didn't respond.

"Look, Mrs. Stuben, somebody's going to do this, it might as well be me."

She sputtered, bristling with indignation. "I think Bluebeard used that line, too."

Anger singed the edges of his control. Why did these people hate him? He was doing them a favor. Without him, they'd have nothing. Didn't they understand that? He kept his expression respectful, tried to be reasonable. "It's just a business. You can always start another one."

She gasped, eyes glistening with affront. "How can you be that callous? To me, this carcass you're so casual about tearing apart wasn't *just* a business. It had a heart and soul." She stood straight and proud, trembling with impotent rage. *"Mine!"*

He watched a lone tear channel a rivulet through the soot on her cheek. His gut went sour, his mood veering sharply toward pity, but he fought the feeling with all his strength.

"For your information, *Sir*—"

"The name's Mitchell Rath, Mrs. Stuben," he cut in. "Call me Mitch."

The hurt and anger in her emerald eyes slashed at

his protective barrier like barbed wire but he managed to preserve his composed mask. "For your information, *Mitch,* those textiles I designed were hand-made works of art. My seamstresses and I were painstakingly bringing them to life on fabric *I* designed. I'll have you know they were worth four times what you paid!"

"They were worth what you could get for them," he countered. "To be honest, you were lucky I found anybody who'd take those things."

Her lips dropped open. From her aghast expression, he knew he might as well have told her she had ugly children.

Claire's smile was gone now, and she looked upset. Apparently she, too, had been stung by his "those things" remark. *Good going, Rath,* Mitch told himself. *Now for some really big laughs, go rip the wings off a few butterflies.* "I'm sorry if I offended you," he said, meaning it. "I'm sure they were—very beautiful."

"Don't bother to apologize, Mr.—Mitch." Elaine tugged on her aunt's hand. "You're right. They were just *things,* worthless and useless, no matter how lovingly they were created. And the money you paid me was just enough to allow me to compensate my workers. Thank you *so* much."

With her aunt in tow, she made it to the door before she halted to glare at him. They were close now. He could detect her scent, a vague whiff of flowers, coupled with the smell of fireplace soot. The combination made a singular impression on him. So did the fury in her eyes.

"Have you ever known the joy of creating something unique and beautiful, Mr. Rath?" She paused only a beat. "Whatever kick you get from the bloodlust of destruction is a pitiful substitute for *real* contentment.''

He extended an arm, clamping his hand on the opposite doorjamb to block her exit. He was tired of sparring. It had been a long day, and he was at the end of his patience. ''We can debate my contentment or lack of it some other time. Right now, I have a proposition for you, and I don't intend to let you walk out on me again before you hear my offer.''

''Offer?'' Claire asked.

Mitch glanced at the older woman, her ruddy features inquisitive. When he turned back to Elaine, her expression was deeply suspicious. '''Offer?''' she echoed, sounding skeptical. ''Our business is finished. I have nothing left to loot.''

Her infernal references to thievery galled him, but *blast it,* he needed her. He couldn't let his pride and her animosity short-circuit his plans. ''If you choose to use the term 'loot,' let's use it.'' Holding his temper in check he spoke quietly, evenly. ''For allowing me to loot two weeks of your time and expertise, I might be willing to let you keep this.'' He extended his arm to indicate the mansion.

She followed the sweep of his hand, then eyed him with distrust. ''Keep—the—the house?''

He nodded, watching her face. He could practically see the wheels whirring out of control. She couldn't fathom what he meant.

''I don't understand,'' she breathed, almost too quietly to hear.

He knew that from her incredulous expression. He also knew that second by second she was forming grave doubts about what sort of expertise she had that would buy back a multimillion dollar estate. Her features hardened. Her eyes went wide, conveying fury and shock. "Are you out of your—"

"No, Mrs. Stuben," he interrupted. "I don't intend to—*loot*—your body, if that's what you're thinking."

Elaine's cheeks burned with humiliation at his accurate guess about the indecent conclusion she'd jumped to. He pursed his lips as though to hide a smirk. She could almost hear him thinking, *Why, Elaine Stuben, what a dirty mind you have behind that dirty face!*

"Please explain exactly what you mean, Mr. Rath," Claire said, fluttering like a protective, though ineffectual, mother hen before the Big Bad Wolf.

Elaine heard her aunt's question, but couldn't take her eyes off Mitchell Rath, looming there, blocking her escape. Dark eyes glinted. His chiseled features held sensuous sway over her, and she couldn't seem to move.

How could she despise this man, yet be incapable of pulling her gaze from his? Rakish good looks were no excuse for surrendering one's principles! She grappled with her self-control and her good sense. "Yes," she finally managed, her voice raspy. "What exactly do you mean? What offer?"

He lounged against the door frame, one hand clasping the jamb near her. He looked so cool and unflappable, yet somewhere beneath that surface she sensed a restive energy. Though his expression, his body language, were the epitome of cold, calculating reserve, under the surface he was generating enough erotic heat to melt the polar ice caps. Against her will and better judgment this strange incompatibility and inconsistency in his character drew her, intrigued her.

Looking into those eyes she was once again struck by his deliberate isolation, his don't-get-too-close vibe.

It was almost as though Mitchell Rath resented her. *He resented her?* She wanted to laugh out loud at that crazy notion. Obviously his nearness was affecting her like an electrical power station, causing interference, making her thinking processes go staticky.

"It's simply this, Mrs. Stuben," he said, breaking into her unsettled thoughts. "I want some face time with the great Paul Stuben. As his daughter-in-law, you have access and influence. Get me a meeting with the man and I might allow you to keep this house."

"My—my heavens," whispered Claire. "That's quite a thing to say."

Elaine agreed with her aunt's astonished comment and stared at Mitchell Rath. This twist threw her for a loop. "A—a meeting?" she repeated, still attempting to assimilate his words.

He lifted his hand away from the door and crossed his arms before him. "It won't be as simple as it sounds. I've tried to get a face-to-face with him for a month. The great leader of Stuben Department Stores refuses to take my calls."

His offer was sinking in now and she shook her head. "Well, if it's a meeting with Paul Stuben you're after you don't want my help. He hates me." The recollection of her distraught father-in-law's harsh accusations came rushing back. She slumped against the wall, dropping eye contact. "He blames me for Guy's death."

No sound came from Mitchell Rath. Elaine kept her gaze lowered, watching her hands clasp, unclasp and reclasp. Another stab of depression cut deep. She knew she was being ridiculous to take his charges to heart. She would never have wished Guy to die. But the very day she'd planned to tell him it was over...*that very day he died.* She couldn't shake the sickening sense of responsibility.

"It's true, Mr. Rath," Claire softly filled the gap. "Guy died in a plane crash. He built the contraption from a kit, an experimental aircraft. Elaine only suggested he get a hobby. She had no idea he would pick anything so dangerous as—"

"He doesn't need our life history, Aunt Claire." Elaine reluctantly lifted her gaze to meet Mitch's. To save her husband's ancestral home would be something she'd do in a minute if she could, no matter how hard she had to work. But her father-in-law's hatred, his crushing grief over Guy's death, well, the division was too insurmountable, literally etched in stone—a gravestone. "I can't be of help to you. Paul Stuben hasn't spoken to me since Guy's funeral."

Mitchell Rath's features hardened in a blatant declaration of his displeasure. "I see." As he ingested this bitter pill his cheek muscles bunched, giving his square jawline dramatic impact.

Among the conflicting emotions Elaine experienced as she watched the display was a surge of satisfaction. Before her eyes the villain in the last, sad chapter in the death of her company was suffering a defeat. She imagined witnessing such a moment in Mitchell Rath's life would be the privilege of only a handful of individuals, and should be cherished appropriately.

Her euphoria didn't last more than a few heartbeats before Mr. Rath's expression changed.

With the suddenness of a slap, Elaine found herself confronted by a smile, so sexy, dazzling—*and scheming*—she shivered with downright dread.

CHAPTER THREE

"You may not be one of his favorite people, Mrs. Stuben," he said. "But you have access. For instance his country club? Isn't that right?"

"I suppose, as a member of the fam—"

"And you get invitations to the same parties and charity events?"

"Well, yes, from time to—"

"And, you do want to keep this fine old home, so you don't have to move?"

She could never stay here now. After all, had Guy lived, she would have been long gone. She could never think of this mansion as hers. But she would love to see the place stay in the Stuben family. If she could save the estate to help make amends to Paul Stuben—well, she'd give anything to do that.

But Mr. Rath didn't need to know the details. He would just interrupt with another argument before she could explain, anyway, so she nodded, remaining mute.

"Then you can be of help to both of us."

"Lainey," Claire interjected. "It can't hurt to try, can it?"

Elaine flicked her gaze to Claire then back to Mitchell Rath. She felt like he'd dropped her from a great height, leaving her dizzy and bruised. How could he continue to dangle the manor before her like a carrot in front of a hungry rabbit, demanding the impossible as though it were simple? Didn't he get it? She shook her head as much to search for words this money-grubbing tyrant would understand as to make her feelings plain. "Listen to me! Both of you! Paul Stuben *hates* me. He would no more listen to anything I had to say or trouble himself to meet anybody I was with than he would—kiss a rattlesnake!"

"Don't be too sure," Mitch said. "Word has it that he's been doing some bizarre things lately."

"What are you saying?"

"He's making bad business decisions, acting eccentrically. Throwing fits at board meetings. Haven't you heard the rumblings that he's teetering on mental collapse, intent on bringing down his empire?"

Elaine could only stare in disbelief. "No…"

"Lainey hasn't seen her father-in-law in months," Claire said. "She has nothing to do with the department stores, and certainly hasn't had money for shopping sprees."

"I haven't seen Paul since Guy's funeral," Elaine murmured, recalling how rude and irrational he'd been right after Guy's death. She still bled from his accusations. Had his grief and bitterness caused his mental health to suffer? Was her father-in-law so lost in sorrow he would willfully destroy a century-old department store empire, famous for its refinement and good taste? "Is that even possible?" she whispered aloud.

"It's happening."

She shot Mr. Rath a perplexed look, having lost the thread of their conversation. "What's happening?"

His eyebrows dipped as though he thought she was so feeble-minded she couldn't follow a simple discussion. Naturally he would think that. After all, hadn't he just bought the leavings of her late, lamented company? Biting resentment shot through her at the reminder that he had something she wanted badly, something she had loved and nurtured with her heart and soul. Something he didn't give a flip about!

"The board of directors is nervous," he went on. "They're afraid he's going to run the firm into the ground. If he does, I want to be at the head of the line to buy out what's left."

His blunt admission appalled her. "You—you want to use me to help you get first chance at the leavings? You actually think I'd be party to such a contemptible plan?"

"Face it, Mrs. Stuben." He eyed her levelly. "If your father-in-law has had a breakdown, and if the worst happens, somebody's going to swoop in to pick the carcass clean. When he loses everything, do you want to have lost the family home, too? Wouldn't you prefer that *I'm* the vulture doing the swooping? At least, that way you'd still have a roof over your head."

"He has a strong argument," Claire said, looking imploringly at her niece.

Elaine tasted bile at the awful idea and swallowed several times to rid herself of the taste. "That's blackmail!"

His chin lifted a notch, almost as though her accusation stung. Or was that brief impression of distress a figment of her overwrought imagination? His features remained composed. "It's just business, Mrs. Stuben."

"Lainey?"

Elaine shifted toward her aunt, but continued to glare at Mitchell Rath for another beat before she could drag her gaze away. "What is it, Aunt Claire?"

"I know it's none of my business, and Mr. Rath is well-known to be a ruthless businessman." She flitted a sheepish glance at him. "No offense meant."

His sober half nod was his only response.

Claire faced Elaine. "But he's right when he says it's just business. Why even in the quilting game I've run up against a few old biddies who would rip out your heart for your last fat quarter of calico." She made a sad face. "Like I said, it's none of my business. I only want the best for you."

She touched Elaine's cheek with affection. "I'm going upstairs so you two can talk." She glanced at Mitch. "I'm sure you're hungry. There's a chicken salad sandwich on the counter and milk in the fridge." She headed out the door, adding, "Elaine hasn't had a bite all day, and when she misses a meal she's grouchy. Eat. Both of you. You'll feel better."

Before Elaine could grasp her aunt's outlandish counsel and even more outlandish suggestion that her worst enemy join her for supper, the older woman had disappeared.

The silence became so deafening Elaine could hear the distant drip-drip-drip of a faucet.

"Maybe you'd better eat." His baritone voice echoed in the cavernous kitchen.

She sharpened her glare. "Even a full stomach would not improve my attitude toward you."

His glance lifted from her and he looked down the hall, apparently following her aunt's departure. "It couldn't hurt."

She fisted her hands, the desire to punch his nose so strong she had to physically press her arms against her sides to restrain herself. "I would rather chew nails."

Resuming eye contact with her, he pursed his lips, the pause long. If he were anybody else, Elaine would have thought he might be counting to ten to hold on to his temper. "Whether you eat or not while I'm here is your business, but I intend to show Paul Stuben my good intentions," he said. "Let him see me as a magician rather than a predator. All I ask is that you make it clear you're pleased with how I've helped you."

"*Pleased* with…how you've *helped* me?" She rolled her eyes, hoping the theatrical move would make the absurdity of his suggestion abundantly clear. "You don't need me, Mr. Rath. You need an actress with no moral fiber."

His jaw muscles did their sexy-bunching act again, so Elaine forced her gaze to the knot in his fancy tie.

"I think I'll eat," he said, removing himself from her glare.

"You—you'll what?" she stammered. When she managed to break free of her shocked paralysis, she spun to watch him walk to the kitchen counter. He indicated the plates of food. "Any preferences?"

She found herself choking out a scornful laugh. "Yes. That you *leave*."

A dark brow rose a fraction before he broke off eye contact, picked up half of one of the sandwiches and took a bite.

"You're actually eating my aunt's supper?" She stalked over to plunk herself in front of him, hands on hips. "You're really going to do that?"

"I'm hungry," he said. "I haven't eaten all day, either." He pulled up a kitchen stool and sat down, holding the half sandwich in her direction. "This is very good."

"I know it's very good. I made the chicken salad."

He took another bite, his lips curving slightly upward. She wondered if it was a minimal smile of appreciation for her culinary talent or merely the way his mouth worked when he chewed.

Exasperated that this gate-crasher was actually making himself at home, Elaine refused to succumb to her hunger pangs in front of him. She tried to ignore the growling coming from the general location of her belly and prayed he couldn't hear it.

He stood up and headed for the refrigerator. The suddenness of his move unsettled her and she stumbled back a step. "Look," he said over his shoulder, "you might as well get used to me and quit cringing. I'm not going to do you any physical harm." He gave her an odd look, as though curious about the earlier manhandling comment she'd let slip. Her cheeks heated. It was true, in the final few weeks before Guy died, she had become afraid of him. His unprovoked, jealous rages had been escalating. He hadn't become physically abusive, *yet*, but she'd sensed—feared—

"However, I do plan to be here until I get that meeting with your father-in-law." He turned away and opened the fridge. After a couple of seconds he pulled out a plastic milk container, glancing her way. "Where are the glasses?"

She indicated a shelf beside the stainless refrigerator.

He grabbed two tumblers, returned to sit on his stool, then filled both glasses with milk. Shoving one in her direction, he began to eat the other half sandwich.

"Are we completely at home, now?" Sarcasm edged her question.

"Not completely," he said, then finished off the sandwich.

"Really? What a shame. Please tell me how I might make your stay more enjoyable."

"I could use a shower." He picked up his glass and watched her reaction over the rim as he downed the milk. Did she detect mockery in his tone? The bum was making fun of her, enjoying her slack-jawed outrage.

Furious he'd turned her gibe to his benefit, she made a guttural sound, something between a growl and a shriek. "You are rude, crude and lewd, sir!"

He set down his glass with a *thunk*. "You are stubborn, foolish and you suffer from an excess of pride!" He shoved the sandwich plate toward her. "Eat. Your aunt can show me to a room. Tomorrow, when you've had some rest and food…" He cast his gaze over her in a thorough, frowning inspection. "…and you've had a chance to bathe, you'll be in a more reasonable frame of mind." He took his plate and glass to the sink and ran water over them. "You'll see your options for what they are. Either lose everything to me, or help me. If you decide on option two, you have a chance to keep this property."

He opened the dishwasher and deposited the dishes inside before facing her. "Not to mention its sentimental value. I understand your husband's mother and grandmother were born here." He stood there, Mr. Dressed-To-Kill with his California tan, long wet fingers curled around the stainless-steel counter edge.

He looked like a *Gentleman's Quarterly* ideal in that high-priced suit and power tie, tall, dark and threatening, in the sparkling kitchen. Yet all of a sudden something about him was different, less forbidding. What? His hands? Wet with dishwater? That was the only thing that had changed.

"Good night, Mrs. Stuben," he said, though his gaze continued to probe hers.

Instinctively she fumbled for a nearby dish towel and tossed it to him. "Good—good night." She didn't know why it was important to her that he dry those hands. Did she want him to be threatening? Surely not.

He took the towel, wiped his hands, laid it aside and walked out.

Elaine stood there in a daze. After the tapping of his hand-stitched shoes died away, the only sound she could detect was her grumbling stomach. Mitchell Rath, in his baffling act of domesticity, had turned the faucet handle so it no longer dripped. She stared at the silent faucet, then at the sandwich and glass of milk waiting on the nearby countertop.

She didn't know which concept was more bizarre—the fact that he'd poured her a glass of milk and tidied up his dishes, or that he wanted her to make nice for him with her hostile father-in-law.

Soul-weary she perched on the kitchen stool. With a sigh, she propped her elbows on the counter, resting her head in her hands. Mitchell Rath was a calculating pirate—who did his own dishes. She closed her eyes. "So what if he has a few manners?"

Somewhere in her head a comparison emerged. In all the time she'd been married to Guy, she'd never seen him tidy up after a meal, or serve her a glass of anything. Of course he'd been brought up in the lap of luxury. He'd been accustomed to being waited on and catered to. Elaine had no idea about Mr. Rath's upbringing. Evidently somebody had taught him the basics of good breeding. "But that doesn't change the fact that Mr. Mitchell Rath is a blackmailing bastard."

"What doesn't change the fact that I'm a blackmailing bastard?"

His voice boomed in the silence, though he hadn't spoken loudly. Whirling around she almost fell off the stool. "I—I thought you'd gone!" It was one thing for

him to know how she felt, but another entirely for him
to hear the offensive B-word from her lips. She winced.

His expression gave away nothing. "What doesn't
change the fact that I'm a blackmailing bastard, Mrs.
Stuben?" he queried again. The man was like a broken
record about getting answers.

She felt terrible about using gutter language. She
never did! This breach of her code of conduct was an
obvious sign the stress was getting to her. Indicating
the sink, she admitted, "You rinsed off your dishes."

He watched her for a moment, seeming to take in
her remark and the incredulous way she'd stated it. The
slight crease of his forehead let Elaine know he was
surprised she would find fault with that small, civil act,
along with everything else about him. "That was my
parents' doing." His lips twisted sardonically. "Over
the years I've managed to unlearn *most* of what they
taught me. Forgive the lapse."

She felt the lash of his mockery and stiffened her
spine. "Really! How fortunate that you've managed to
defy *most* kindly urges." She tossed her head in defi-
ance. "What did you come back for, or do you make
a habit of eavesdropping on the mutterings of your
prey? You must love pain!"

"I love pain as much as the next man." He approached her. When he loomed large, she shifted away.
He noticed her visible rejection and frowned, though
this time he refrained from remarking on it. He merely
scooped up the sandwich plate. "I came back because
I decided to take this to your aunt," he muttered. "You
won't mind eating something else, right?"

She didn't respond, just glared. He'd seen the inside
of the refrigerator. Did the fact that there was nothing
in there but half a jar of pickled beets and three apples

cross his selfish, self-centered consciousness? She suppose she could fix herself a bowl of oatmeal and slice an apple over it. He was never going to hear from her lips that there was no chicken salad left, or hardly anything else for that matter.

Still, she wondered why he was taking the meal to her aunt. "She won't be so easily swayed to your side, you know."

"But you're sure I'm ruthless enough to try."

His cynical remark stopped her cold and she could only stare.

He indicated the upper floors with a small gesture. "Where's her room?"

"At the top of the staircase," she offered slowly, trying to figure his angle. "Turn left." She pointed in the general direction, grimly wishing she could break into his thoughts. Read his conniving mind. "First door on your left."

He nodded, flicked a tiny cell phone from his inside jacket pocket and handed it to her. "I'm still hungry." He fished out a leather wallet and produced a platinum charge card, tossing it on the countertop. "Order a pizza. I hear Chicago is world famous for it." He returned the wallet to an inside jacket pocket, lifted the milk glass and turned away.

He'd nearly reached the door before she could lift her gaze from the phone he'd placed in her hand. "Er—what toppings do you want?"

"Your choice." He shifted to look at her. "Order whatever you think a vulture would appreciate. Only keep in mind, you'll be eating it, too." His gaze held hers for an instant longer, then he was gone.

She frowned after him. Had that parting shot been pure sarcasm or was he actually buying *her* supper?

Had he noticed the bareness of the refrigerator after all, or was he merely concerned with filling his own belly?

Elaine was bewildered, and she didn't like the feeling. Were these seemingly kind acts as cunning as he implied, or were they the result of the burdensome thoughtfulness ingrained in him by his parents?

She looked down at the charge card and picked it up, fingering it. Considering the fact that she'd made no secret of her dislike, he was being amazingly trusting, leaving her alone with his platinum charge card! Perplexed, she clutched it, shaking her head. The man was a disturbing mix of all-business aloofness and open-handed gallantry.

Taking no chances this time, she hopped off the stool, tiptoed to the kitchen door and peered down the long, empty hall. He really was gone. She slumped against the wall and stared at the phone in one hand and the plastic charge card in the other. "Okay, Elaine," she muttered, "So he's a *gallant,* blackmailing bastard!"

CHAPTER FOUR

ELAINE ate half of the deep-dish pizza and Mitchell Rath had still not returned to the kitchen. She wondered what he'd been doing all this time, hand-feeding Claire her sandwich? If he was so all-fired hungry, he wasn't acting much like it.

She was stuffed. Even if it were the best pizza in the world, she couldn't get another bite down to save her life. She stared daggers toward the empty kitchen door. If he thought she was going to hang around here until he decided to amble back in, he was crazy.

She shut the lid on the pizza box and scooped it up along with his charge card and cell phone. She wanted to be rid of him and his belongings. The only way she could be sure to get it done on her terms was to hunt him down and shove them at him.

She tromped up the stairs and hurried to her aunt's room. Since her hands were full she knocked lightly with her toe.

"Yes?"

"Aunt Claire, is Mr. Rath in there?"

"Heaven's no." She sounded sleepy. "I'm in bed."

"Do you want me to take your dishes downstairs?"

"Good grief, no, Lainey. I'll do it in the morning. You get some rest."

Elaine readjusted her burden when the phone started to slip. "Uh—well, okay. What room did you give Mr. Rath? I have—er—he ordered a pizza."

"Oh?" Elaine heard a yawn in the word. "That's nice. He's in the one next to you."

"Next to..." She couldn't quite believe what she heard, so the last word came out in an incredulous squeak. *"Me?"*

"It's the nicest room with southern exposure. Being from California, he's not used to our cold winters. I thought he'd be most comfortable there."

"And why would we care to make him *comfortable?*" What was wrong with her aunt? Didn't she see the man for the bandit he was?

"What, Lainey?"

"I said—"

She heard a throat being cleared and whirled to see the bandit himself approaching along the hall. The sounds of his footsteps were muted by the Oriental rug runners, so he was too near to have missed her last remark.

He'd changed into jeans and a faded red sweatshirt with the gold, block letters University of Southern California splashed across his chest.

"What?" Claire called. "I couldn't hear that."

"She said she appreciated your making me comfortable, Claire."

"Oh? Fine. I told you she'd be in a better humor after she ate. Good night, Mitchell. Good night, Lainey."

"Good night," he said, apparently for them both, since Elaine couldn't manage to do more than glare at him.

His hair was a little mussed, as though he hadn't smoothed it back after pulling the shirt over his head. That surprised her. She'd assumed he spent his free time preening before a mirror. That tousled, breezy look didn't fit in with her image of him.

"Let me help you, Mrs. Stuben." He relieved her of his phone and credit card, depositing them in trouser pockets. "I gather you didn't eat any pizza."

"I ate half of it," she said. "I told you my attitude toward you would not get any better, even on a full stomach."

"Ah, right." He nodded, as though just recalling the statement—

Like he'd forgotten! No way! She shoved the box at him. "I hope you like pineapple-onion."

She wasn't sure if the guttural sound he made was his reaction to her choice of toppings or a result of the box being heaved into his solar plexus.

"A fruit and vegetable pizza?" His eyes glinted his displeasure. "I'm sure it will be—nutritious."

She felt that stunning impact of his aggravation in the pit of her stomach—a hot jab that nearly buckled her knees. Sucking in a breath, she shifted her gaze away. Scrupulously avoiding eye contact, she made a big production of brushing imaginary pizza crumbs from her sweater. "Well—I'll be off to bed. I have a long day tom—"

"We start in the morning, Mrs. Stuben."

That statement halted her in midword. Perplexed and mistrustful she pivoted to stare at him. "'Start'?"

"Where will Paul Stuben be in the morning?"

The totality of the man's ability to focus on his objective boggled her mind. Ever since his disquieting exit from the kitchen she hadn't given one instant's thought to her father-in-law. She didn't like to think any emotion but her loathing of Mr. Rath had taken hold, but she feared the thrust of his square chin and the length of his astonishing lashes may have intruded upon her thoughts—once or twice. That made her angry. If he could be single-minded in his scheme to use her to get to her father-in-law, she could be just as single-minded in abhorring him with every fiber of her being! To Hades with his square chin and sexy lashes!

"Mrs. Stuben?" Hearing him call her name snapped her from her dark thoughts. "In the morning, where will your father-in-law be? At his office?"

She shook her head. "He usually plays golf on Friday mornings," she admitted grudgingly. "But with the snow, he'll be at the club playing cards with his golf buddies."

"Then so will we."

She wasn't jarred by that statement. She expected it. No doubt single-minded determination to reach a goal was how he'd gotten where he was. She closed her eyes and sighed. "This is *not* going to work."

"With that negative attitude, I'm not surprised your company failed."

Her eyes flew open. "My attitude had nothing to do with the failure of my company. And it's no business of yours, but I'm very optimistic by nature!"

Murder in her heart, she stomped toward him, but for some reason she stopped short of giving him the kick in the shin he deserved. She had no idea why. Maybe it was the fifty pounds he had on her. And kicking a man who could crush you like a bug was unwise to say the least.

Or maybe it was the fact that Guy had come frighteningly close to physical abuse. The idea that she could even consider behaving in the same way agitated her. "Keep your opinions to yourself, Mr. Rath!" she muttered, working to regain her self-control. "You have no idea what you're talking about."

He observed her for another couple of seconds before he nodded. "You're right, Mrs. Stuben. I apologize." His nod looked like a dismissal. "Good night."

He passed her and walked to the end of the hallway to vanish inside his room. His door closed with a solid thud. Sadly, that door was a mere yard from her own. She stood there vacillating for a long time—three minutes, possibly five—before she realized how silly she was acting. He wasn't *in* her room, just next to it. The walls were thick. She didn't have to worry about him bursting through them like some kind of anti-superhero.

She headed down the long hall, grumbling that her aunt had rocks in her head for her intolerable decision to place this man in the room next to hers. There were eight other perfectly respectable bedrooms she might have chosen, though none had the precious southern exposure his discriminating California sensibilities seemed to require.

Her thoughts careened back to his blackmail scheme. It was so despicable she hated the thought of being a party to it, even if she could save the mansion from his grasping clutches.

A thought struck. What if Paul Stuben got himself under control and didn't run his company into the ground? If that happened, even if she went along with the awful plan, Mitchell Rath's manipulations would only be a waste of his time—clearly the commodity most precious to him, next to the almighty dollar. She chewed her lip. What would happen then? If she did everything Mr. Rath asked of her, would she still lose the house? The only reason she was considering the plan was for her father-in-law's sake. The estate should revert to him if it went to anybody.

She reached her door but couldn't quite turn the knob. Not until she knew. She had no intention of going through with one single lie or the smallest deception if there was a chance she would lose the estate to Mitchell Rath. She'd rather surrender it honorably now than turn into a collaborating worm and lose it anyway.

Determination bolstered her resolve, and she rapped on his door. The sound was louder than she expected, her anger and righteous indignation lending weight to her knock. Her knuckles throbbed with the punishment.

He didn't answer, so she pounded with both fists, insistent that he respond. "*Mr. Rath!* I need to talk to you! *Right now!*"

"Okay, okay," came a deep voice, sounding aggravated. "I'm coming."

She planted both fists on her hips, allowing herself a smug smile. She liked aggravating him. It gave her a crazy sense of power. Almost relishing the confrontation, she lifted her chin, composing the requirement she would insist be added to their deal. "Mr. Rath," she murmured, practicing. "If I do everything you ask me to, I *demand* you abandon any right to this estate, no matter what the outcome is between you and Paul Stuben." Yes, that sounded good.

The door swung wide. Elaine opened her mouth, but her prepared speech exploded into unrecognizable bits, banging and clanging around in her head and clogging her throat, until the only noise she could force out was, *"Gug?"* It sounded like a question, which it probably was, since her scandalized brain was screeching, *Why are you wearing nothing but a towel?*

He crossed his arms over a broad chest dusted with

dusky hair. "That's very entertaining, Mrs. Stuben. But couldn't it have waited until morning?"

Her gaze roamed downward from his chest, past a delectable navel to the sea-green towel secured rather precariously at his waist. She'd seen the bath towel before, since she'd recently laundered it, wanting everything to be fresh before she left.

As she recalled, it was a big towel, at least she'd thought so when she'd folded it. But scanning it now, Elaine noticed it skimmed barely halfway down thighs, muscular, tan and taut. She was unsettled to discover there wasn't an unappealing scrap of flesh on the man, or a less-than-fascinating contour beneath the green terry.

Inwardly she cursed the towel for the skimpy excuse for cover it was. As she stared, she grew concerned that her silent cursing might be aimed at more than the paltry bath towel. She *might* be cursing herself for her inability to keep her gaze from wandering on down to take in long, athletic legs, with just the right amount of brawn, sinew and manly hair.

"Is 'Gug' Chicago shorthand for 'the house is on fire'?" he asked. "Or did you forget to wish me sweet dreams?"

At the sarcastic note in his voice, she blinked hard, coercing her attention to his face. He stared her down. "Uh—" She'd lost her train of thought. All she could see in her head was a green towel that didn't disguise his masculine attributes nearly enough. She felt clammy and twittery at the sexy vision that refused to leave her mind's eye.

What was the matter with her today? Anyone would think she'd never seen a grown man in a towel before! Just because her life with Guy had become a dismal,

sterile existence. Just because every spark of love had
been systematically crushed out under the heel of his
domineering was no excuse to get hot and bothered
by—

"Would you care to come in?"

Shocked by his assumption that she wanted anything
from him other than his head on a platter, she spat, "I
would rather be attacked by a pack of wild boars!"

"Than by a bore wearing a towel?" he finished the
thought for her, though it hadn't entered her mind.

Thank heaven for his wicked suggestion and sarcastic taunt. Or had the wicked suggestion also been sarcastic? It didn't matter. Either way it slapped her brain
back on track. "Absolutely," she said, more under
control as her animosity reasserted itself, centering her
on familiar ground. "I knocked on your door because
I want to make one thing clear—Mr. Rath." She found
it hard to refer to him so formally, considering he was
nearly naked. She shook off the thought. It was better
she keep her mind and her eyes off his lower half. Or,
for that matter, his upper half!

"Uh—" She licked dry lips, focusing on his left ear.
"I came to inquire—if I do everything you ask of
me…" That sounded uncomfortably lewd considering
his recent proposition, so she hurriedly added, "That
is, if I do everything you ask of me in your scheme to
make points with my father-in-law, and he still won't
deal with you, do I lose the estate?"

Her query caused his gaze to narrow. He watched
her for a moment, as though actually giving her question serious consideration. "Hmm," he said. The quiet
that followed was unnerving.

She sucked in a breath. It felt quivery. She was not
nearly as poised as she looked. At least she hoped she

looked poised. "Think hard, Mr. Rath," she warned, breaking the strained silence. "Because if your answer is no, I refuse to be part of your scheme. That's all I intend to say on the matter."

He watched her with those dark, probing eyes, his demeanor cold-blooded. At least as cold-blooded as anyone could be without a stitch on. That chilly stare notwithstanding, there was still way too much heat radiating from that scrumptious male body, and Elaine's cheeks burned with the effect.

"Well," she croaked, masking her unease with bravado. "I'm waiting."

He lifted a single eyebrow and his lips pursed for a heartbeat. "You drive a hard bargain."

She didn't respond, afraid to trust her voice.

"But—I have faith in myself." His lips lifted vaguely. "And in your father-in-law."

She experienced a tingle of trepidation at his tone, and frowned. Did he mean he had faith in her father-in-law's ability to see his side of things, or faith that the old man was careening down the road to certain mental collapse, and would ultimately have no choice but to sell out?

"So, no matter what the outcome, I get the estate?" she asked in a near whisper, hoping against hope.

"If…" He unfolded those arms, exposing that marvelous chest to her full view. "*If* you do everything I ask of you."

She angled her gaze to his ear, the one on the right this time. "You won't ask me to do anything illegal—or against my moral code?"

He didn't speak for a moment, which confused and worried her. She couldn't help but shift her gaze to his face. He was observing her with undisguised skepticism. "Exactly what would violate your moral code, Mrs. Stuben?"

Her instincts bridled that he would dare ask such a question. Hadn't she made herself perfectly clear? Was he being obtuse simply to embarrass her? "You know exactly what I meant."

"I'm afraid not," he countered, his expression impassive.

She suppressed her fury at him for forcing the issue, very sorry that she'd brought it up. Apparently any breaching of her moral code or of anything else about her person had never entered his mind.

The hardest thing she'd ever done was to meet his gaze. But she did. To mask her squeamishness, she glared with a vengeance. "I won't sleep with—with *anyone*."

Her declaration hung in the air between them. Mitch looked her straight in the eye until she couldn't help but look away, uncomfortable. "You seem preoccupied with sex, Mrs. Stuben," he said, at long last. "If I were you I'd seek therapy about that."

His reproach stung and she met his gaze defiantly. "Who invited whom into whose room?" she threw back.

So there!

"Blast it, woman," he said gruffly. "You looked pale. I thought you might like to sit down."

"Yeah, sure!" she scoffed, but her theory that he'd been making a pass faltered. "I'm not the one preoccupied with sex, mister! It's *your* dismal moral code I'm dubious about. I want to make sure—"

"I thought I'd been clear that your virtue is safe with me," he cut in. "I need your assistance, not your wild abandon, or even your affection."

She made a guttural noise she'd never heard herself make before. It had to be the sound that comes just before smoke billows from a person's ears. She was incensed and mortified. The rage she understood; the mortification baffled her. Why did his assurance that she was not capable of inciting a man's desire bother her? "Well," she said, hurting and wanting to strike back. "For your information, Mr. Rath, you'll never, *ever,* have my affection!"

His brow creased for a beat, then his expression grew cynical. It was almost as though he'd thought about it and noted she'd left out any mention of "wild abandon."

"Wait a second!" She plunged in to correct any misguided notion that she would *ever* consider wildly abandoning herself to him. "I didn't mean—"

"Don't panic." He took a step back into his room. "If there's any wild abandoning to be done, I'll let you go first." He dipped his head in a scant bow. How was it possible for him to be chivalrous and shamelessly mocking at the same time?

"But—"

"Sweet dreams, Mrs. Stuben." As the door closed between them, he added, "Be ready by nine."

Mitch hadn't slept well, though he could find no fault with the room or the bed. It had been quiet. Not too quiet. Perfect for slumber, but he'd tossed and turned. "If there is any wild abandoning to be done, I'll let you go first?" he mumbled, incredulous at himself for saying such a stupid thing. He poured a mug of steaming coffee. What had been in his head when he'd said that? One loose screw, at the very least.

Had he really been concerned for her health when

he'd invited her into his room? "Said the spider to the fly," he muttered, taking a sip. She hadn't believed him for one second and he didn't blame her. Though he wanted to be that unaffected by her, he was kidding himself if he thought he was.

She couldn't be more transparent about how she felt about him. If anybody in the history of the world hated anybody more than she hated him, he'd—he'd... "I'll eat that withering pineapple and onion pizza, sitting on my bedside table."

"Did you say something to me, Mr. Mitch?"

He turned at the sound of Harry's voice, and replaced his frown with a friendly smile. "Yeah, buddy. Ready for more pancakes?"

The redheaded youth with the backward baseball cap grinned. "Do they have nuts this time?"

"Yep."

"Then, sure. I never had pancakes with nuts before."

"It's a specialty of mine." He laid his mug on the counter and skimmed three more pancakes off the griddle onto a serving plate.

"This is so nice of you, Mitch." Claire smiled up at him as she poured maple syrup over her stack of pecan pancakes. "All these groceries and cooking breakfast, too?" Her smile radiated in her eyes, the same pretty green as her hostile niece. "What a lovely surprise to wake up to."

"I don't really like to order take-out pizza for breakfast, so I figured groceries would be a good idea." He served Harry his third helping of pancakes and paused by Claire's chair at the kitchen's stainless-steel table. "More coffee?"

"If you don't mind." She handed him her mug.

"But remember, Lainey and I do the dishes. It's only fair."

"You've got a deal."

He took her mug to the counter and refilled it. Retrieving his own, he returned to the table. "Here you go."

"Now fix yourself a plate, Mitch." Claire patted the white plastic cushion on the metal chair beside her. "Sit down, relax."

He went back to the griddle, pushed his sweatshirt sleeves to his elbows and flipped the three other pancakes that were midway through the cooking process. He checked his watch. Eight o'clock. Apparently the quarrelsome Mrs. Stuben intended to deprive him— *them* of her company until the very last minute. He had a fleeting thought about her hair, wondering if she planned to uncover it for this morning's trip to the country club.

He wondered how long it was. Chin-length? Shoulder-length? Longer? And what did it feel like— all that golden-red stuff? Silky, he bet.

What the— He was actually contemplating the feel of Elaine Stuben's hair? Was he crazy? *Keep your mind on business,* he warned inwardly. *Securing the Stuben empire will be a billion-dollar coup. You need the woman's help, so keep your eyes on the prize! Like you said, she's not here to ease your lust. She's here—full of reluctance and outrage—to help you snatch—*

"What's going on?"

Mitch didn't need to turn around to know who'd asked the sleepy question. He was sorry to detect an escalation of his heart rate with what he feared might be arousal. *Down boy,* he told himself. *She detests you. And you told her you had no designs on her. Try to keep that in mind.* So what if your fitful dreams were chock-full of visions of wide and willing moss-green eyes, her red-gold hair spilled over silken sheets... Remember why you're here. Paul Stuben's department store empire would be the crowning achievement of any entrepreneur's professional life. You'll be American royalty—with wealth and power beyond your wildest dreams. *Focus!*

Even after the stern lecture to himself, when he shifted around his glance shot to the doorway.

There she stood, in a baby-blue terry robe and matching scuffs on her feet. A mass of red-golden hair dipped a few inches below shoulder-length, framing her face in a disheveled corona. She looked like she'd just slipped out of bed, a sweet-and-sexy handful of woman. *Lord!* He suppressed a feral growl. She was more irresistible than she'd been in his dreams.

Why was this woman making him so hot? The forbidden fruit syndrome? Was it the fact that she wanted nothing to do with him that made her look enticing? He liked a challenge, but the business venture that had brought him to Chicago was challenge enough.

Her gaze met his and the engaging, heavy-lidded bewilderment vanished, replaced by an all too familiar scowl. His mood plunged, unfortunately his state of arousal didn't.

"Good morning, Lainey," Claire said cheerfully. "Join the party." She lifted her coffee mug toward the gas rangetop where he stood. "Mitch made pecan pancakes for breakfast. They're delicious."

Elaine's gaze slid to her aunt, scanned the table set for four, then darted back to his face. The scowl didn't ease. She rubbed her eyes with the backs of her hands.

It was almost comical, as though she didn't believe
what she was seeing.

She scuffed further into the kitchen, looking droopy
and tired, as though she hadn't slept well. Her artfully
disarrayed hair sparkled in the fluorescent lighting.
"Where did all the food come from, Aunt Claire?" she
asked, clearly ignoring Mitch. Halting at the corner of
the table between Harry and Claire, she leaned heavily
on the surface with the flats of her hands and looked
at the youth. "To what do we owe the pleasure of your
company, sweetie-pie?"

He swallowed a bite and grinned up at her. "Mr.
Mitch needed groceries. Mom works the early shift today. I go in with her on cold days, since the school's
close to the supermarket. When Mr. Mitch called, I
offered to package everything up. Willie, a night cash-
ier, brought me and the groceries over on his way
home. When we dropped 'em off, Mr. Mitch invited
us for breakfast, but Willie had to get home." Harry
took a big gulp of grape juice, leaving a purple mustache above his mouth. "Mr. Mitch is gonna give me
a ride to school in his cool car."

"He is, hmm?" Elaine peeked at Mitch, frowning.
When she gazed at Harry again, her expression soft-
ened. "You look like Groucho Grape, my man."

"Huh?"

She touched his upper lip with a fingertip and Mitch
could almost feel the caress against his own face. He
ran the back of his hand across his mouth.

"Your purple mustache," Elaine said with a grin at
the boy.

Harry still looked confused.

"Remember that Marx Brothers's movie I rented for

your birthday last month? Groucho was the one with the funny mustache.''

"Oh, yeah." Harry grinned. "He rocked."

"Well, young man, you have a funny purple mustache."

Mitch smiled at the cozy little scene of a happy family unit around the breakfast table, then caught himself. *Cozy! Get a grip, Rath. You're an unwelcome house guest fixing breakfast for a few near strangers, not making home movies!*

Harry giggled and wiped his mouth with his shirtsleeve.

"Oh, no you don't!" Elaine looked pained and picked up the paper napkin beside his plate. "Use this, kiddo. Grape juice stains are *not* fashionable this year."

"Oh—yeah." Belatedly the boy swabbed at his mouth, tossed the napkin down and took up his fork to dig into the pancakes. "These are great pancakes. They rock."

Elaine lifted her gaze to Mitch, her dubious expression returning as she straightened. He'd suppressed his sappy grin and merely stared back, trying to appear nonchalant. She pushed a mass of fiery curls out of her eyes, the better to glare at him. "They're rocks, huh?"

For some demented reason he found her muttered insult amusing. Hell if he knew why. Maybe it was her contrary spunk. People who'd lost everything usually felt like losers, were unsure and down on themselves. Not Mrs. Stuben. She was feisty, argumentative, passionate and stubborn.

She only resembled others he'd bought out in her resentment toward him. He, Mitchell Rath—The Vulture—had success *and* power *and* money. Those who'd failed had nothing, and after his buyout, they

didn't even have the business they'd nurtured and
loved.

Mitch had grown accustomed, even calloused, to the
embittered attitude. Strangely, he found it hard to be
calloused where Mrs. Green Eyes Stuben was concerned.

He didn't feel pity for her. Far from it. He felt an
all-consuming sexual attraction, and it made him vulnerable, a character flaw he'd fought all his adult life.

She walked around the table, grabbed a mug down
from a shelf and poured herself a cup of coffee. Leaning against the counter, she peered at him.

He experienced a shiver of pure lust at the peek-a-
boo thing her hair was doing, exposing one eye. He
imitated her posture and lounged against the counter
beside the rangetop. She wasn't far away. At least not
physically. Trying to get his attitude adjusted from
lusty to steely, he lifted his mug in a small, mocking
salute. "You're not a morning person, I see."

She pushed the wayward lock of gilt-auburn hair
away from her face. As she mimicked his cynical salute, it tumbled back over one eye. "And you're not a
person I care to see in the morning."

He sipped his coffee to mask a wry grin. *Touché,
Mrs. Stuben,* he threw out telepathically. *You look cud-
dly and sexy in the morning and you have a sharp wit!
Quite a package!*

"Now, now, Lainey," Claire said, looking upset. "I
thought you two had come to an understanding."

"We have, Aunt Claire." Her peek-a-boo glower remained on Mitch. "We understand that we don't like
each other."

Elaine passed in front of him and gave the griddle

and its contents a once-over, then went to a nearby cabinet and pulled out a container of dry oatmeal.

"What are you doing?" Claire asked.

"Fixing breakfast." She set down her mug and rummaged in a cabinet under the counter, retrieving a small pan. Coming back across his path to the sink she filled the pan with water. "Excuse me," she mumbled, retracing her steps in front of Mitch to deposit the pan on the gas burner furthest from the griddle, which only left them a foot apart.

"I'm guessing you don't like pancakes," Mitch said, catching a whiff of her hair, light, flowery, but this time without the acrid slap of ashes. He tried to dismiss the thought, but found it impossible. *Blast it!*

"I like pancakes just fine, Mr. Rath." She didn't look up as she fished a measuring cup out of a drawer. "It's *you* I don't like. And I don't want your charity."

"You can't live on oatmeal for the next two weeks," he said, trying to be reasonable.

She shifted to stare at him, her eyes glinting with resolve. "Care to make a bet?"

His amiable attitude evaporated. Only a fine line separated determination and bullheadedness. Elaine Stuben had just crossed it. Annoyed, Mitch walked around her to the oatmeal box and looked inside. Not much left. In stony silence, he emptied the entire contents into his pancake batter.

"What do you think you're doing?" Elaine cried.

He stirred the dry cereal into the batter. "I'm having oatmeal and pecan pancakes for breakfast."

"But—but that was all I..." The sentence trailed off. Mitch flicked a glance at her.

"Was it?" he asked, pretending innocence. "Sorry."

Her cheeks grew crimson. "You are not sorry! You're a thief and you'd stoop to stealing a person's last mouthful of food!"

"Are you two fighting?"

The question came from Harry. He sounded upset, and younger than his twelve years. Mitch wondered if his mother and father had fought just like this and if such a similar display frightened him.

"No." Mitch turned to grin at the boy. "We're having a difference of opinion. Adults do that."

Harry scrunched his features, looking worried and pugnacious. "Don't be mean to Miz Elaine," he said. "If you make her cry—I—I won't be your friend."

Mitch experienced a stab in his belly. Harry was clearly fond of Elaine and in his twelve-year-old way was aggressively protective of her.

"Oh, sweetie-pie." Elaine hurried to the table, removed his Cubs cap and gently stroked his hair. "Mr. Rath is right. We were just having an—adult—er—difference of opinion." She replaced his cap and took his worried face in her hands. Mitch felt a perverse jab of envy. "It's all over now, sweetie." She looked at Mitch and smiled, or more correctly bared her teeth. "I think I will have some of those—*delicious* pancakes, thank you."

Mitch took her cue. "Great idea. Coming right up." He smiled back, his expression equally forced, but surely delivered with a thousand times less antagonism. He removed her pot of steaming water from the burner and scooped up three pancakes. Depositing them on a serving plate, he took them to the place set for her. "Hot off the griddle," he said, his grin less forced. Catching a glimpse of slender leg as she gathered her robe about her and took her seat alleviated a chunk of his hostility.

"Thank you," she gritted out, that fake smile plastered on. Her eyes flashed with animosity. Mitch wondered if her expression fooled Harry. Surely he knew a real smile from "Miz Elaine," and this was *not* it.

"You're welcome. I hope you like them."

"I'm sure they're—fine." She picked up the syrup pitcher and drizzled the stuff over her hotcakes.

"Orange juice or grape juice?" he asked.

She sucked in a huge breath, didn't look up, but nodded. "Orange—please."

After he'd served her, he made himself a batch of pecan and oatmeal pancakes. Okay so maybe he'd been a jerk about the oatmeal. But one thing he hated as much as the fear of being a sucker for every sob story that came along was dealing with a stubborn fool.

He skimmed up his pancakes and turned off the griddle, then took a seat across from Claire. Elaine sat on his right. He checked his watch practically under her nose. Eight-thirty. He had time to eat, get Harry to school, then change into a suit.

He didn't miss Elaine's furtive glance. She frowned at his watch. He knew she knew he was reminding her about their nine o'clock date.

He ate silently while Elaine and Harry and Claire chatted about the forecasted snowfall. Claire looked over and smiled at him every so often, and he forced himself to smile back, but remained out of the weather discussion. Elaine made a point of looking everywhere but at him. He was sorry he knew that. Obviously he was doing way too much looking at her.

When an elongated silence took over, he lay down

his fork and turned to Harry. "Well, bro, are you about ready to head off to school?"

"Sure," he said, gulping down the last of his grape juice.

Claire patted her lips. "I promised Mitch we'd do the dishes, Lainey." She stood. "Don't hurry, though. I'll start working on the griddle."

Harry's chair made a screeching sound on the white tile floor as he scooted away from the table. Gathering his plate, utensils and glass, he carried them to the sink.

"Thank you, sweetheart," Claire said with a smile as she rolled up the sleeves of her green plaid shirt. "Oh, your tip!" She fished in her pockets, then looked upset. "I'll have to go upstairs and—"

"Claire, they were my groceries. I'll get the tip." Mitch retrieved his wallet and pulled out a five. "Here you go, Harry."

The boy walked from the sink and took the bill. "Thanks, Mr. Mitch," he said, his attitude slightly subdued. Mitch had a feeling the boy was debating whether he should get too close to this man who had the power to make his darling "Miz Elaine" unhappy.

"You're welcome," Mitch replied and stood. "Let's get you to school." He felt guilty about upsetting the boy and hated himself for giving a damn. But for the next two weeks he had to look like a friend of these women. To help that fiction along, he lay his hand over Elaine's resting on the table and squeezed gently in an aren't-we-good-friends manner. He dipped toward her and murmured, "I'll see you around nine, Elaine?"

She dropped her fork with a clank. Her wide eyes met his and he gave her a quick, cautioning signal by darting a look at Harry. With any luck she'd think he was doing the good-friends thing to alleviate the boy's anxiety. After a split second's hesitation, her lips lifted in a tremulous smile. Lady luck was still with him. "Oh—sure—Mitch. Nine." She nodded. "I'll be ready."

"Great." Against his will he recorded the fact that her hand was warm, her skin soft. He found himself lingering, squeezing again. A beat later Elaine slid her fingers free to take up her orange juice glass. She also broke eye contact first. Plainly she'd reached her limit pretending to be his friend, even for Harry's peace of mind.

"We'd better go, Mr. Mitch." The boy tugged on his sweatshirt sleeve, sounding back to normal, his chipped grin, spontaneous and disarming.

"Right, Mr. Browne. But first let's fix that hat," Mitch teased. "It's all wrong." He plucked it off by the bill and resettled it sideways on the boy's head. "There. That's better."

"Ah—you're real funny, dude!" With a chortle, Harry swung the bill to his nape. "Race ya to the car?"

"Yeah, sure. Whoever wins gets to unlock it with the remote." He tossed the keys in the air.

"Oh, boy!" Harry snagged them with one hand and sprinted out of the kitchen.

Mitch strolled after him. In the hallway he found himself lifting his hand to his face, inhaling her scent.

His smile died.

CHAPTER FIVE

ELAINE and Mitch drove in tense silence to Avalon Glen. Over the years the stately golf and tennis club had been the recipient of many large contributions by the Stuben family. Mitch informed the gate guard that his passenger was the wife of the late Guy Stuben. The uniformed sentry looked in the car and immediately smiled with recognition, having seen her many times when she and Guy had attended the club.

She felt sick to her stomach, unsettled by the possibility of a confrontation. Restless, she watched as the gate swung open, the guard admitting her with all the pomp and circumstance befitting the widow of a fallen prince of Chicago society. She'd hoped Paul had put out the word never again to allow her to darken the door to "his" club. No such luck. Here she was getting in way over her head on Paul Stuben's turf, about to see him face-to-face. She didn't want to think about what the next half hour would bring.

The antique-filled gaming room was nearly empty on this blustery January day. Outside the arched picture window, gray sky spit snow; inside, cigar smoke coiled in the air like ghostly snakes. The stench hit Elaine's nostrils and made her gag.

Elaine coughed behind her hand, glancing anxiously around. She clung to the hope that for once her father-in-law had decided to stay home. Her wish was not granted. There he sat, at a table of four men, across the richly paneled room. Behind them a rustic stone hearth served as a massive focal point. A fire crackled and blazed in its depths.

She pulled her lips between her teeth, strangling another cough. *Keep it together, Elaine,* she cautioned herself. *No matter how you feel, or what Paul thinks, you are not responsible for Guy's death. You have nothing to apologize for! Guy was no saint, and though Paul has a right to grieve, he doesn't have the right to condemn you!*

The white-haired gentlemen at the leather-topped card table were engrossed in a game of poker, idling away their time until the winter weather ended and their Friday mornings could again be spent on the club's manicured links.

She stumbled to a halt two steps inside the room, her legs mushy. It took all her strength to remain standing.

Mitch asked in an aside, "Which one is your father-in-law?"

She shook her head, trying to clear her vision. She wasn't breathing very well. She coughed against the back of her hand. Her lips seemed hot against her cold hand.

"What's wrong?" Mitch whispered. She could feel his gaze on her. "Are you sick? You look green."

She flicked him a glance, sucking in a smoky breath. It didn't help her roiling stomach. "I'm peachy," she croaked.

He frowned. "Don't pass out on me."

She frowned back. "Your concern is heartwarming." She didn't know which was harder on her, staring into the midnight eyes of the man who was blackmailing her, or at the man who hated her with a fierce passion.

How well she remembered that profile, the straight patrician nose, jutting chin and thick, wavy gray hair. Sadness squeezed her heart and she winced. He was a handsome man in his early sixties. With a disquieting mix of melancholy and stomach-churning aversion, she recalled how much Paul and his son resembled each other.

Upon closer scrutiny, since the last time she'd seen him, he seemed to have lost weight. Belatedly she remembered Mitch's query about which one he was, and indicated him. "Paul's on the left," she murmured through a strangled cough, "in the gold cardigan and navy trousers."

Mitch didn't respond so she assumed he was sizing up his quarry. All Elaine heard was the hissing sizzle of the fire and low rumblings of the men as the poker hand was played out. The cigar smoke stung her eyes and made her queasy, but she trudged resolutely into the lion's lair.

Paul lifted his brandy snifter and drained it. Without looking up, he snapped his fingers in the air. "Reggie! I need a refill."

Out of the corner of her eye, Elaine saw a man wearing black and maroon approach the table carrying a bottle. He poured a brownish liquid into Paul's snifter. As he straightened to leave, Paul thrust a hand out and grasped his forearm. "What's the matter with you, Reggie. Fill the cursed glass."

The man murmured something that sounded apologetic and splashed more brandy into the snifter.

Elaine had a bad feeling. Paul Stuben had never been a daytime drinker. And it was only nine-thirty in the morning. The other men also had drinks. Two held coffee mugs, and at the elbow of the third sat a tumbler of orange juice.

Mitch drew her out of her musings when he took her elbow and coaxed her forward. "You're on, Mrs. Stuben."

"Don't *push!*" She tugged from his grasp. *"I'm going."*

"Do you know the other men?" he asked near her ear. She detected his warm breath against her cheek. He smelled of a cedar forest and strong coffee. The pleasant combination somehow helped relieve her queasy stomach, reminding her of overnight hiking trips Claire had taken her on as a girl. But this man was no pleasant stroll in the forest. He was a blackmailing pirate, and she'd better keep her head on straight about that.

"Do you recognize them?" he asked, catapulting her back to the task at hand.

"Oh—er—yes. The man across from Paul, the one with the bushy eyebrows, sucking on the cigar, is Marlon Breen. He's on the Stuben board. So is the portly man with the hair combed over his bald spot, Cal Landenburg. I don't know the other man. Probably some woebegone golfer."

Mr. Woebegone was the first to spot them, since his chair faced the door. He held his cards close to his chest and asked in a nasal voice, "Can we help you?"

At that point the other three men took notice. Elaine knew the two member's of Paul's board of directors would recognize her. She didn't know how much venom they would spit. Her father-in-law hated her thoroughly and without limits. As far as how badly his hatred had infected the others on his board, well, she would soon see.

She sucked in a breath polluted with foul smoke and coughed. Though her stomach churned, she cleared her throat and made herself smile. "Hello, Marlon, Cal." She nodded politely, noting their expressions were more surprised than repulsed. Marlon even took the smoldering cigar out of the corner of his mouth and returned her smile. "Hello, Elaine."

She nodded an acknowledgment, her glance skidding to her father-in-law. "Hello—Paul." The greeting came out amazingly composed, considering her unease. "It's been a long time."

The initial glance he'd given the newcomers quickly ended. He glared at the cards in his hand, looking as though he had no intention of responding, so she hurried on. "Gentlemen, I'd like you to meet a—a friend of mine." She had a hard time saying those fraudulent words without gagging on them, but there was so much at stake. To save the Stuben mansion for Paul, she would call a venomous snake her best pal—which wasn't all that different from what she was doing.

"This is Mitchell Rath." She indicated him with a nod and a glance, struggling to maintain her cordial expression. "Mitchell, meet my father-in-law Paul Stuben—and Cal Landenburg and Marlon Breen." She faced the lone stranger. "I'm sorry, I don't—"

"*I fold.*" Paul slammed his cards down hard, startling Elaine. His features rigid, he sliced a murderous look at her. His dirt-brown eyes were full of rabid anger. "I have to make a phone call, gentlemen." He cut his glance away as quickly as he'd hit her with it. She felt like she'd been slapped.

"Excuse me," he growled, grabbing his snifter. Vaulting up, he swayed unsteadily and seized the chair for support.

Elaine moved to aid him. She took his arm to help steady him. "Are you feeling all right, Paul?" she asked.

He gave her a deadly look and growled, "Get your hands off me!"

"Paul, please," she began, needing to reason with him. "I'm not your enemy. Let me help."

"We'd both like to help," Mitch added, drawing up beside them.

Paul eyed Mitch, his hatred for Elaine clearly transferred to her companion. Without a word, Paul released the chair, moved the glass to his free hand, then yanked from Elaine's hold. Listing right, then left, he shuffled to a side door that read Men's Locker Room. An instant later the slam of the door broke the tense quiet.

Paul's intoxication upset Elaine and she found her anxiety replaced by pity. With difficulty she dragged her attention from the locker room door to the men seated at the card table. All three stared bleakly at the exit. They looked upset.

After a sickly pause, they turned to stare at Elaine, the movement so synchronized it was creepy. She shook her head. "I'm sorry if I broke up the game."

The other men shrugged, mumbled.

Mitch cleared his throat. "This is my fault."

"Not at all, Rath." Marlon blew out a stream of smoke and Elaine found herself holding her breath. "Stuben's been—well, don't take it personally, son."

"That's kind of you." Mitch thrust a hand toward the cigar-chomping man. "It's good to meet you. I'm a long-time admirer of the Stuben operation. I hope to meet Paul Stuben—when he's—in a better frame of mind."

Mitch moved around the table, shaking Cal's hand,

then that of the elderly, bespectacled third man. Elaine didn't catch his name. She was too busy watching The Vulture swoop in. The fact that he'd admitted his culpability in Paul's discomfort amazed her. He was smooth, she had to give him credit. He'd gone right into his act, buddying-up, pretending to be oh, so sympathetic and solicitous. *Ha!*

He looked like a take-charge executive in that perfectly tailored navy suit and conservative, striped tie. His clothes, though traditional, oozed subtle elegance. She wondered if this Midwest Banker look was part of his ploy to "fit in," to shout, *I'm just another conventional good-old-boy success story, like you.* If this physical guise was half as successful with these elder Chicago capitalists as it had been with the female staff and guests of the club, he was well on his way to victory.

Except for one, tiny complication. Paul Stuben was gone.

She felt faint and realized she was still holding her breath. She gulped air with way too much smoke, and broke into a coughing fit.

"Elaine?" Mitch said. "You're not looking well. Would you like to get some fresh air?"

His remark surprised her. He *knew* she was anxious and upset. Why the sudden concern? "Excuse—me?" she asked through a cough.

"I said, would you like to get some fresh air?"

"I'd love some," she said tightly. She was suffocating and sick at heart. She had suspected Paul would be unpleasant, but she never guessed he would cut her dead with his look. "If you're ready to go, I'm ready," she said.

"Elaine," Marlon said, "My daughter, Tiffany, is

here with her baby. She's in the grill having coffee. I'm sure she'd love to see you. Why don't you visit with her.''

Elaine thanked Marlon with a smile and was about to decline, when the older man shifted to look at Mitch. ''While Elaine visits Tiffany, why don't you sit in for a hand or two, Rath?''

Mitch grinned. ''I haven't played poker since college,'' he said, looking almost believably modest. *Almost!*

''Then it'll be a pleasure to take your money, son.'' Marlon set the deck of cards in the empty spot. ''It was Paul's turn to deal.''

''Well, if you insist.'' He took Paul's vacated seat.

Elaine didn't understand what Mitch was doing. This was a twist she hadn't expected. Maybe he hoped Paul would return. She knew he wouldn't and couldn't imagine Mitch Rath being so naive as to believe he would. Possibly he knew it but decided by smoozing with Paul's cronies, he could get them to put in a good word. Or maybe he just liked poker.

Whatever, at least the time he spent at cards would give her a breather. She needed to get out from under the influence of his looks. Ever since he'd returned from taking Harry to school, he'd looked at her funny. The silent inspection made her so uneasy she wanted to scream. ''Okay—well...'' she murmured.

Mitch picked up the deck and began to shuffle. ''Forgive me if I'm rusty.''

She watched him handle the cards. He didn't look rusty. He glanced her way. ''Was there something you wanted to tell me, Elaine?''

She shook her head. What was she doing, staring at

the man! Why wasn't she running headlong out of the noxious good-ol'-boy's hideout? "No—I'm going."

"Have a good time," he said as he began to deal. "I won't be long."

"Take your time." She turned away. *Have a good time, indeed! Who was he trying to kid with that daddy act?*

Relieved at the chance to escape his watchful eye, she hurried away. She loved babies and she would enjoy seeing Tiffany's. Her heart lurched. She'd wanted children, too, but all too soon those dreams had been dashed. She could never bring a child into a world ruled by Guy Stuben's unmerciful, iron fist.

An hour later Elaine sipped a ginger ale in the grill, alone at the table she and Tiffany had shared. Mother and baby had left for an appointment with the pediatrician, but Elaine lingered. She had no intention of returning to the gaming room to fetch Mitch. He could just come find her.

"Well, I won."

She looked up to see the man she least wanted to see in the universe. He seemed taller, if that were possible. Much to her distress, he was a striking picture standing there. The overhead wrought-iron light fixture graced him with just the right illumination to enhance the width of his shoulders, the prominence of his cheekbones and the sweeping expanse of his lashes. She took a shuddery breath and lowered her gaze to study the table. "What did you win?"

He seated himself to her right, drawing her hesitant gaze.

A waitress came over to the table. "What can I get for you, sir?"

"Coffee," he said, then returned his attention to

Elaine. "I won fifty cents." He chuckled, the sound deep and unfamiliar. She reacted with a tremble of appreciation she wished she didn't feel. "Those captains of industry are reckless gamblers."

Elaine found the subject far from amusing. Along with Guy's other faults, he had also proven to be a reckless gambler. She hadn't discovered until after his death that he'd gambled away his trust fund. When he'd magnanimously offered to pump money into her e-business for the big deals he'd gotten her into, little did she know he'd mortgaged the family home to do it.

Guy had been such an egotist and so in need of being Mr. Wheeler-Dealer, he'd not only overtaxed her company with contracts she couldn't fulfill, but stupidly jeopardized the last asset he had. Not only that, but his insurance policy listed his father as beneficiary. Guy never bothered to make the change, no doubt assuming he would live forever. Due to his colossal ego, his rash behavior and his gambling compulsion, he'd left her drowning in debt.

"It was a joke," Mitch said. He seemed in an unusually buoyant mood, considering how huge today's failure had been.

"I got the joke. I just didn't think it was funny." She took a drink of her ginger ale. "Congratulations on the fifty cents. I know money-grubbing is your main thrust in life. I just thought today's mission was buddying up to my father-in-law."

The waitress brought a steamy mug and placed it in front of Mitch. "Cream or sugar, sir?"

"Nothing, thanks." His gaze remained on Elaine's face. "That was the plan." He took a sip of coffee, watching her over the mug's rim. She began to feel that troubling prickle again. His attention was too probing, too deliberative. Though he hadn't asked anything, she felt as though she were being interrogated. He set down the mug. "You're going to have to do better than you did today."

She didn't appreciate the threat in his tone. "I told you what would happen. You're lucky he didn't toss that glass of brandy at us."

"I noticed he took it when he left." His eyebrows rose for emphasis. "He was pretty fried."

Elaine couldn't deny it. "I saw." She leaned forward, placing her forearms on the white linen. Absently she fingered the diminutive crystal bud vase that held one, perfect blood-red rose. "He didn't used to drink like that."

"He didn't used to do a lot of things."

Out of the corner of her eye, she saw Mitch take another mouthful of coffee. She turned away to stare out of the multipaned window displaying a snow-covered golf course, dotted with pines and oaks, their boughs weighed down with snow.

"So Guy made you cry?"

She frowned, positive she'd heard wrong. Twisting around, she stared. "What did you say?"

He shifted to better face her. She felt the nudge of his leg against her knee and experienced an unwanted thrill. Hurriedly, she crossed her legs to avoid his touch.

"Harry told me Guy made you cry," he repeated, his tone confidential. "He talked quite a little bit about you and your late husband."

A searing stab cut deep and she closed her eyes with the memory of those demoralizing times, enduring

Guy's irrational ranting. When she opened her eyes, his expression was unreadable, his gaze searching.

Taking stony control of her emotions, she said, "I don't care to discuss my husband with you."

He lounged against the table, resting an arm on the linen cloth. "Harry loves you, you know." The only indication that they weren't discussing the forecast was the fact that he leaned toward her, whispering, "He warned me not to make you cry—like Guy did."

Embarrassed to have been the subject of discussion between Harry and this man, she looked away, absently watching the waitress in black and maroon carry a tray to a couple having brunch. She blinked several times, determined to get herself together.

"Did he hit you?"

"*No!*" Elaine's head snapped around, and she glared. It was true Guy hadn't hit her. But he'd come close, and she'd sensed it was only a matter of time. That's why she'd been packing, having made up her mind to walk out, when she got the news of his death. "I said I don't want to discuss—"

"Is his bullying why you're so antagonistic toward me? Because you refuse to be a carpet for any man to walk on, ever again?"

She glared him down, but her deadly look didn't cow him the way she wanted it to. He simply watched her, unblinking, unmoving. His relentless regard made it difficult to catch her breath.

She tried to find words that would thwart his inquisition, but the look on his face told her no language existed that would work. She attempted to dodge the subject. "It's not complicated, Mr. Rath. I'm antagonistic toward you because I don't like you."

"So you've said." Though his lips crooked in a deceptively genuine smile, his eyes told her the truth, flashing with anger. "Luckily, I only ask that you pretend fondness for me."

Uttered quietly and through a dazzling but dishonest smile, anyone looking at them would think he was complimenting her eyes or her hair. She floundered around in her head for a biting comeback, but nothing came. Why did his smile, even as twisted and cynical as it was, short-circuit her ability to think?

"So, your husband made you so happy you cried?" he asked.

His persistent sarcasm offended her. Okay, so maybe she had overreacted *somewhat* to Mitch because of Guy's bullying and controlling. Maybe that's why she and The Vulture continued to clash, no matter that he'd bought her dinner and badly needed groceries. Or that he'd cooked a wonderful breakfast. Every time they crossed paths she'd been as shrewish as she could possibly be. She had to admit, some small portion of her anger might be a direct result of Guy's tyranny.

Mitch was perceptive to suggest her overreaction was due to a knee-jerk defense mechanism—having promised herself *never* to be trod on by any man again.

In her own defense, Mitchell Rath had come to Chicago with the undisguised intent to tread all over her, first with his Master of the Mansion attitude, then by blackmailing her into his scheme. What did he expect her to do, kiss him for buying her out for pennies, then pressuring her into his web of deceit?

"What if he did make me cry?" she finally admitted. "You think you're so different?" Her question was hushed but hard-edged. "If Guy was controlling and bullying, I'd think you'd see how I might be *slightly*

rebellious at being pushed around by another controlling bully!''

His brow furrowed. He looked away, out of the window, but she had the feeling he saw nothing of the
wintry scene. His cheek muscles bunched, flexed. Had
she hit a nerve? She sat back, dully watching him.

She couldn't believe she'd admitted Guy's abusive
behavior to this man. She never intended to tell anybody! Not even Claire knew the whole truth, though
she was too intelligent not to have sensed things had
been bad almost from the first.

Mitch's reminder that Harry had witnessed her pain
brought back the memory with a vengeance. Elaine
squeezed her eyes shut, trying to block out the recollection, but it rushed forward, ruthless and remorseless.
She'd been so shamed when Harry caught her during
one of Guy's tirades. She remembered exactly what it
had been about. Recalled every stinging word—how
Guy had reminded her for the hundredth time how he'd
so gallantly plucked a local girl in cheap shoes from
the rabble and how he was offering to teach her so-
phistication. He'd shouted, ''How can you ever be part
of well-bred Chicago society if you don't align your
shoes according to season, and subcategory them by
color!''

Furious with her ''slipshod'' closet, he'd thrown
each shoe, one by one, out of their second-story bedroom window, punctuating every throw with cruel con-
demnations. Then he'd screamed at her to go outside
and get them. How dare she litter the lawn!

Disgraced and frightened of his temper, she'd retrieved them, her humiliation witnessed by the entire
household staff. Guy always made sure they observed
her punishment. He seemed to need an audience no

matter how inappropriate the situation or how humiliating to those around him.

Elaine had been unable to hold back tears as he'd bellowed from the upstairs window how hopelessly déclassé she was. Harry had come peddling up on his bike just then. He'd seen her driven to tears, her arms loaded down with the shoes *Guy* had bought for her. Shoes she couldn't stand to wear and had given to charity mere days after her husband's death.

She felt pain in her hands and realized she'd balled them into fists. Her nails sliced into her palms. She rubbed her hands together under the table. "Look, I'm going home. I have work to do. I'll catch a ride to the elevated train." She planted her hands on the linen cloth, preparing to push up from the table. "Don't worry about your coffee. I've signed for it."

He stood and walked around behind her to help her from her chair. When she stood, she saw him toss a ten dollar bill on the table.

"I told you—"

"I know what you told me." He motioned to the waitress and she hurried over, a smitten little smile on her face. The woman was plainly as enamored of him as the coat check girl and sundry other women who'd seen him since they'd arrived. "And you'll ride the 'L' home over my dead body."

"Yes, sir?"

"This is for our drinks and your tip."

"But Mrs. Stuben already—"

"Tear it up. They're on me."

"Yes, sir." The woman scooped up the bill, gushing, "Thank you, sir."

Elaine felt his hand graze the small of her back as he walked with her to the front entrance of the stately club. The gallantry surprised and troubled her. However light the contact, the sensuous heat it generated was disturbing.

At the coat check room, he extracted the tickets for both their coats, paid the attendant a handsome tip and assisted Elaine into her wool jacket. She endured his courtesies in frosty silence. He'd already admitted they were ingrained and meant nothing.

"I'm sorry about your husband," he said.

She glanced at him, dubious. "Sorry about what?"

He opened the door for her and she preceded him out into the biting chill. He handed his parking stub to the attendant who skittered off to fetch his Mercedes.

"I'm sorry he was such an ass," Mitch said, once they were alone.

She experienced a lurch in her chest. She had never dared allow herself to think such a negative thought about Guy. Somehow it seemed if she did she'd have to admit her mistake, making such a sorry choice for a life partner.

How defective must her ability to judge people be to have allowed her to be so blind to Guy's shortcomings? That was another reason she was frightened of her attraction for Mitchell Rath. How demented must she be to feel flutterings for another abominable human being! And unlike Guy, Mitchell Rath wasn't even trying to hide his polluted character. Was she insane?

She heard a bitter, unsettling laugh, made even more unsettling when she realized it had come from her own throat. "Yeah," she said. "I seem to be a magnet for men who are asses." She looked at him, positive he couldn't miss the dark message in her eyes, that shouted, *You are just like him!*

He looked skeptical. "Are you calling me an ass, Mrs. Stuben?"

She poked out her chin, defiant. "Whatever would give you an idea like that?"

He nailed her with a chilly look. "That's what I thought."

Elaine watched the snow flutter down outside. From what she could see in the glow of the bronze yard lamp, Chicago had been blanketed with another three or four inches since she and Mitch left the club.

She had managed to avoid his company the rest of the day by keeping busy boxing up personal items in the room she'd used as her business headquarters. She checked her watch. Nine-thirty in the evening. How time flew when you were hiding out. It only seemed like a year since she'd checked her watch fifteen minutes ago.

Tired and hungry, it irked her to need to hide in her own house. Well—she amended mentally—at least it was her house for the next two weeks. Whatever happened after that depended how well she pleased Mitch Rath.

Claire had gone out earlier to have dinner and talk shop with a couple of friends. She would be out till all hours. Elaine hated the idea of being alone in the house with Mitchell. But if she was lucky, he had retired to his room. She could probably hazard stepping out into the hallway. Even if she couldn't be sure Mitch was ensconced in his room for the night, she needed food. After she taped up this last box, she would quit for the day and fix a sandwich.

She snatched up the tape dispenser and started to tape, but nothing happened. "Empty!" she muttered.

"Wouldn't you know." Laying it aside, she pushed up from the rug and left the little office. Taking the stairs two at a time she rounded the corner heading toward the back of the house, and rushed down the hallway. Once in the cavernous kitchen, she hurried to the pantry, hoping to find another roll of packing tape.

One under-cabinet florescent light was her only illumination, but it was plenty to get around. She could smell the lingering spicy bouquet of whatever Mitch had eaten for dinner. Spaghetti? Lasagna? Something like that. Her stomach growled, reminding her she must eat. *Soon,* she promised herself. *Very soon.* Inside the pantry, she flipped on the light switch.

Nothing happened. She groaned. The bulb had burned out. "Shoot!" she mumbled. "All I want is a little tape! Does it have to be this hard?"

She pivoted around, hustled out into the kitchen to the shelf where extra bulbs were kept, found a package and returned to the pantry. She lay the bulb pack aside and unfolded a step ladder that stood nearby. Situating it beneath the cut-glass light fixture that covered the offending bulb, she stepped on the lower rung, then stopped. "Oh, a screwdriver."

Back in the kitchen, she rummaged through a hardware drawer until she finally found the right size. Weary and frustrated, she trudged to the pantry and mounted the short ladder.

She could barely reach the fixture that needed removing to get to the bulb, and stood on her toes. She tottered there, straining to turn the first screw. The pressure she put on the screwdriver nearly caused her to topple sideways. She caught herself just in time, took a deep breath of relief and looked around in the semi-darkness. There had to be a better way.

After researching the situation, she decided to brace one foot on the pantry countertop. Lifting her right sneaker to the stainless-steel surface, she stretched up on tiptoe. She felt a little more secure but far from stable. She strained upward, struggling to turn the stubborn fastener. Grunting, she muttered, "I'm going to get you out or die trying."

"Are you speaking to me?"

She was so surprised by Mitch's question, she almost dropped the screwdriver. Easing off her tiptoe, she peered down at him. "It works for you, too, but no. Not this time."

"Can I help?"

He stood in the doorway, clad in a turtleneck and jeans. Even in the dimness the white sweater was easy to see, including some well-defined muscle in his arms and chest. Annoyed that the sight warmed her blood, she shifted her focus to her work. "No, thanks. It's under control." With both hands and all her strength, she torqued the tool—or more correctly, attempted to—but the blankity-blank screw would not budge.

"Why don't you let me take off the fixture for you?"

"Because," she grunted out, forcing with all her might. "I—don't—want—your—help!" Each strained word emphasized another failure to budge the screw.

"I see."

Suddenly, a pair of hands were at her waist, dislodging her from her hazardous purchase. Shocked and disoriented, she yelped, flinging the screwdriver into the air. An instant later, she found herself settled in a standing position. Sadly her legs didn't get the message and she sagged into Mitch, instinctively grabbing his neck.

"What do you think you're doing?" she cried, hugging him with all the power her desire for self-preservation could muster.

"Just—standing here," he said, his tone low and vaguely uneven.

"Just standing here!" she repeated, trying for flip and sarcastic. Unfortunately, the restatement came out soft and breathy. His solid strength gave off more heat than she would have guessed a bloodless automaton could radiate. He felt good. Too good.

His arms came around her, further obstructing her collapse to the pantry floor. "I thought I was averting a concussion," he murmured, hugging her close, his breath tickling her lips.

"I—I was handling it." She suffered the thrilling torment of his nearness, hating herself for feeling anything but anger. Yet even as she berated herself, her heart hammered ruthlessly against her ribcage and she was afraid he could feel the wild pounding.

A quiver of tension coursed through his body. Nestled so intimately in his embrace, she experienced it as though it was a part of her. She hadn't shared anything physical with a man in a long time, certainly nothing as sensuous and stirring as that quiver.

Without a doubt, Elaine knew he was tense because he hadn't expected or wanted her in his arms. Yet even knowing this, an erotic hunger came on in a fiery rush, frightening her in its intensity.

In a sudden flash of insanity, Elaine found herself craving, longing—utterly resolved to be kissed!

By him!

CHAPTER SIX

MITCH hadn't expected to hold the contrary Mrs. Stuben in his arms. He'd expected to hold a screwdriver. His brain did some scrambling to get oriented. Soft, feminine curves pressing against him had an effect he hadn't anticipated or wanted. He inhaled. Her light, flowery scent rushed in with the restorative breath, and his stranglehold on invulnerability slipped a notch.

What was his problem, yanking the woman off the ladder like she was a sack of potatoes? What did he think would happen when he jerked her off her feet? Didn't he know she'd grab the first, solid thing she could find? And that it just might be him?

Had some marauding band of insubordinate brain cells contrived this collision? A sharp stab of guilt pierced his gut. Hadn't he done enough to this woman without turning her into an instrument to ease his lust?

Is that all she is? a gremlin in his brain queried. *Or would you like her to be more?*

He looked into her eyes—pretty, wide and green. She almost seemed to be asking to be kissed. Her lips were slightly parted. So kissable at that angle, her face tipped up perfectly for—

That's a laughable notion, Rath! his rational side argued. *The woman tells you she hates you on an hourly basis!*

Clearing his throat, he fought to wash the lecherous fog from his brain. "Sorry," he said, hoarsely. With an internal curse, he veered sharply away from tricky emotional territory, broke eye contact and set her safely away from him.

For both their sakes he slipped his hands into his jeans' pockets and searched the floor for the screwdriver. "I made baked rigatoni with mushrooms for supper," he murmured, scanning the dim floor. "There's a plate for you in the refrigerator." It wasn't much of an apology, but he hoped it was a start.

She didn't immediately respond, no doubt getting her spleen-venting speech just right.

He spied the screwdriver in a dark corner and retrieved it. Riveting his attention on changing the light bulb, he climbed the step ladder. Even concentrating on the job, the squeak of her sneakers as she exited the pantry didn't escape his notice. The sound retreated rapidly. Before Mitch had the first screw out of the fixture, he knew he was completely alone.

Elaine heard her aunt's light tapping at her bedroom door and called, "Come in." The ornate dresser mirror reflected her face, the model of dejection. Lowering her gaze, she fastened her sterling hoop earring.

"You look so nice," Claire said. "Where are you going tonight?"

Elaine's exhale was a melancholy moan. "The club. It's their annual Winter Wonderland Ball."

"Oh, yes." Claire walked across the antique Chinese rug. Bounding up the four-poster stool to Elaine's high bed, she dropped onto its golden-rose brocade spread like a teenager watching her big sister primp for the prom. "I gather Mitchell wants you to try again with Paul?"

Elaine closed her eyes. Worried about the inevitability of another ugly confrontation, she nodded.

That wasn't the only thing tearing at her insides. Last night's disaster in the pantry nagged like a toothache. Had she actually wanted Mitchell Rath to kiss her? Had she gone that crazy? The only explanation had to be fatigue, stress and hunger. She hadn't been herself these past few days. She couldn't imagine a worse fate than having that man kiss her! How lucky *he* had wanted no part of her and pushed her away. "Lucky," she mumbled, her teeth worrying her lower lip.

"Did you say something, Lainey?"

She shook her head and rubbed her aching temples. "No—nothing."

"He's a darling, isn't he?"

Elaine's eyes popped open. She stared in disbelief at her aunt, lounging there in her jeans and blue flannel shirt, looking perfectly sane. Evidently looks could be deceiving. "I hope you're talking about Harry."

Claire had been examining her fingernails. At the incredulous question she turned her attention to Elaine. "No. I meant Mitchell."

Elaine shifted to glare at the mirror. Her disbelieving expression stared back at her. Behind her own reflection she could see her aunt sprawled on the showy, gilt four-poster. "How can you say he's *darling?* He's making my life miserable. If you call that darling, you're a few crystals short of a chandelier!"

Claire laughed and crossed her legs at the ankles. "All I know is he's been perfectly wonderful around here." She laced her hands beneath her head and looked up at the heavy brocade and velvet hanging that made up the canopy. "Did Guy ever wash a dish or change a light bulb or cook anything?"

Elaine felt herself go rigid, her features taking on a sickly pallor. "Guy was raised rich," she murmured. "He was accustomed to having things done for him." Why was she defending Guy to her aunt? Maybe it was the idiocy of comparing Mitch favorably to Guy that irked her. They were both cast from the same mold. Manipulative, overbearing and egotistical. Just because Mitch helped out around the house didn't make him any prince charming!

"I'm not going to argue with you about this." She abruptly stood and smoothed her billowy, ankle-length cocktail dress. In the mirror she scanned her creation. She'd happened upon the fabric in an out-of-the-way vintage fabric shop and had to have it. The wonderful sheer rose organza, patterned with abstract swirls in salmon-pink, ivory and jade, and woven with diminutive, metallic-silver rosebuds, had made a magical overdress. The slim-fitting slip was a fiery-pink silk.

She recalled how excited she'd been with her diaphanous ensemble when, on their honeymoon, she'd donned it for a night out of dining and dancing. Guy had taken one look at her and insisted the dress was too frivolous for proper society. Crushed, she'd hidden it away in the back of her closet—a garish misdemeanor from her unsophisticated past.

Now, though, she couldn't bring herself to wear anything Guy had bought for her. The memories left a bad taste.

Troubled by the memory, she ran her hands along the transparent scoop neckline and cap sleeves. Anger at Guy's intolerance and browbeating surged inside her. Feeling belligerent, she fingered the demurely gathered, slightly raised waistline, then fluffed the skirt. The gauzy fabric floated freely over the slip-dress and

billowed artfully about her ankles, the torrent of un-
blushing hues accented by delicious flashes of silver in
the lamplight. "I dare you, Mitchell Rath—to give me
grief about wearing this dress!"

"Did you say something, Lainey?"

She shook her head. "No—nothing."

Elaine swept her reflection with proud conviction.
She looked just fine! To Hades with Guy's overbearing,
blue-blooded prejudices!

Another aspect of her attire Guy would abhor was
the fact that she wore no accessories, except the plain
sterling hoops in her ears, a high school graduation gift
from her aunt. The costly jewels Guy had insisted she
show off were long gone to testy creditors, including
her wedding rings.

"I've always thought you looked so good in bright
colors," Claire said, sitting up and planting her feet on
the step stool. "And your hair piled up on your head
like that looks really sophisticated."

Elaine winced at her aunt's use of the word Guy had
pounded into her. *Sophisticated.* She hated that word,
but how could her aunt know?

Claire didn't seem to notice Elaine's discomfort and
made a Maurice Chevalier face, pushing out her lower
lip. *"Trés charmant, chérie,"* she purred in a perfectly
dreadful French accent.

Elaine usually found her aunt's lousy impressions
amusing, but tonight she found nothing funny, or even
tolerable. With each thud of her heart, dismay drilled
deeper and deeper into her chest, making it hard for
her to catch her breath. She only hoped the apprehen-
sion she felt had to do with Mitch's blackmail—*not his
rejection.*

A knock boomed in the stillness. Elaine's heart fluttered wildly.

"It must be Mitchell." Claire jumped off the bed and hurried toward the door.

"Must it be?" she muttered.

Claire checked her watch as she went to the door. "Eight on the dot. He has flawless timing, too."

"Like an execution."

"Hmm?" Claire stopped and faced Elaine. "What did you say?"

Elaine waved a dismissal. "Just—never mind."

Claire's brow knit in confusion for a second, then she shrugged and turned to the door. "Right on time," she said as she let Mitchell in. *"Woooo!"* she hooted in undisguised approval, "Don't you look yummy!"

"Why, thank you, Claire." His voice boomed and ricocheted around the room, an amazing feat, considering he'd spoken in a perfectly ordinary tone.

Elaine fiddled with a fallen curl at her nape, wondering whether she should try to repair it or let it lay. She didn't really care about the out-of-place wisp of hair. After all, hadn't she been in an indignant snit when she'd piled her hair on her head? Flyaway curls already framed her face like a windblown thicket. What was one more fallen strand? The ugly truth was, she simply didn't want to face Mr. Yummy.

"Good evening, Mrs. Stuben," he said. From his voice, she could tell he was still only a step inside her door.

"For corn sake," Claire interjected. "Aren't you two being a little formal? Mitch, meet Elaine. Elaine, this is Mitch. Play nice, you two, I've got things to do."

In the pause that followed Elaine heard her aunt

tromp off down the hallway. She cried out mentally for her to come back, but her aunt's powers of telepathy were nil. The tromping sound grew fainter until it disappeared altogether.

Agitated, Elaine toyed with her watchband. Maybe she shouldn't wear it. The leather band was too informal. She should probably—

"Good evening—Elaine."

His use of her given name touched off an unruly quiver of anticipation and she worked to squelch it. Quivering over this man was out of the question! Mitchell Rath was using her—*blackmailing her*—to feather his own nest. Empty pleasantries should be given the significance they deserve. Absolutely none!

"I see you're ready," he went on. "That dress is— incandescent."

"Yeah," she scoffed, focused doggedly on the marble dresser top. Guy's disapproving image flashed in her mind. "What you mean is, it looks like it was made by a hippie with bad taste!" Feeling her adrenaline pumping, ready for a fight, she shot back, "Well, it was! *Me*."

In the stillness that lengthened between them, the wintry wind howled, rattling the windows.

"Taste is the enemy of creativeness," he said at last, the unexpected remark reverberating through her. She frowned, confused. "Pablo Picasso said that," he went on. "It's rumored the man knew something about creativity."

So what was that supposed to mean? She *did* look like a hippie with bad taste, or looking like a hippie with bad taste was permissible, as long as the bad taste was committed in the name of creativity? Was he mocking her judgment or applauding her inventiveness?

With the bitter tang of resentment on her tongue, she turned in his direction. At first glance, her mind shied like a skittish colt, trying to escape the truth. But no matter how she struggled, she couldn't. *Yummy* was a feeble word to describe the masculine vision framed in her bedroom door. She experienced a shudder at the very heart of her.

He stood there, wickedly handsome, with an air of what Elaine could only describe as brooding dignity. The combination was thrilling and frightening and devastating. The epitome of elegance in his flawlessly tailored tuxedo, his slouchy stance, hands in his trouser pockets, accentuated the musculature of his thighs and the trimness of his hips. Broad shoulders filled out his black jacket to perfection.

The exquisite lines of his formal attire, ebony juxtaposed against the white of his knife-pleated shirt, achieved a minimalist effect that maximized his appeal. He was to-die-for gorgeous, and Elaine's doubled heart rate was painful to endure. When her attention reluctantly lifted to his face, midnight eyes captured her gaze.

Stinging resentment swept over her. How dare he tantalize and frustrate by merely standing in her doorway! What did he think he would accomplish throwing off all that raw sensuality? Not a thing! He was The Vulture, cold-blooded and manipulative. She was too contemptuous of him, too savvy and too discriminating to be affected by such superficial, smarmy allure!

After being on the receiving end of her silent glare for several, tense heartbeats, a strange, half smile twisted his lips. Elaine noted that his dark eyes held no glint of humor. "Now you say, 'Thank you, Mitch,'" he said, "'Aren't you sweet to say so.'"

She experienced a stab at his taunt. "I don't have any idea what you said."

His expression sobered to match the coolness of his gaze as he walked further into the room. "I said you look nice."

"No, you said my dress was *shiny* and Pablo Picasso would be okay with it. I acknowledge Mr. Picasso's genius, but I'm not into cubism. I prefer sensual and emotional art over analytical, fragmented works, though I can see where it might appeal to you. Frankly, I'm *insulted.*"

His expression grew annoyed as he approached. Halting a scant two feet away, he fixed her in an indigo-eyed vise. "Frankly, you'd find a way to be insulted if I said I thought you were the most ravishing creature on earth." Taking her hand, he tugged her out the door. "It's getting late, *Elaine.* You have a chore to perform."

"Yes—*Mitch,*" she said, her tone as clipped as his. "I have to go to a ball with *you.*"

He flicked her a glance, his eyes flashing with annoyance.

Mitch didn't like himself much this evening. He smiled, laughed and chatted about inconsequential things like good movies and bad politics, mixing and mingling in the ballroom with glittery club members. The bank of gigantic chandeliers set on dim, enhanced the romantic ambience, warming the winter's evening with fine food, soft music and courtly surroundings. But romantic ambience or not, fine food, soft music and courtly surroundings notwithstanding, he felt like the world's biggest rat.

Though he hadn't kept Elaine on a short leash, he'd kept an eye on her movements. She'd carried around a plate of delicious delicacies, but touched nothing. Mitch berated himself. Had she lost weight since he'd arrived? Except for a few bites of pancake yesterday morning, had he seen her eat anything? *Great, Rath,* he rebuked inwardly. *She'd rather starve than endure your company.*

He'd given her lots of space tonight, more than he'd originally planned. So far, Paul Stuben had not shown his face. Even so the evening hadn't been a total waste. He'd conversed with Marlon Breen and Cal Landenburg, who'd introduced him to another Stuben board member. Making an end run around the old man might not be as tough as he'd originally figured. Little Miss Elaine, his reluctant date, had done him more good tonight than she could imagine, simply by getting him access to Stuben's haunts.

He lounged against a marble column hardly noticing the swirling humanity on the dance floor. The fact that the orchestra played a tango intruded only slightly into his mind. A glittering figure caught his eye. Elaine swayed into view, held in the arms of a handsome man who grinned at her like a randy baboon.

Mitch surveyed them, his lips pursed in thought. They danced well together. Elaine didn't miss a step, turning and pivoting in the man's arms, sailing right and left. Her diaphanous, twinkling gown drifted about her lithe form like a wispy vapor. He experienced a rush of heat. Had she chosen that transparent getup to taunt him? The damn thing was so sheer it was cruel. And worse, the silky slip clung to her curves, leaving little of her willowy figure to the imagination. Right now, his imagination churned, chewing at his insides. He winced with the realization he was actually jealous of a piece of cloth.

"Blast!" He pushed away from the wall. The tango ended and a slow, sultry melody took its place. He stalked onto the dimly lit dance floor, his target, the twinkling tease-of-a-dress and the diabolical woman who had fashioned it.

With a little more force than he intended, he tapped the baboon on the shoulder. "Cutting in, friend," he said with a smile meant to disarm. Otherwise the guy might think the sharp whack was a challenge to a physical contest for the lady fair.

Ridiculous, Mitch told himself as Elaine's partner gave him a glowering once-over. Apparently deciding Mitch had him outclassed in both height and weight, monkey-boy withdrew.

"What?" Elaine asked, dropping her arms to her sides. "Is Paul here?"

Mitch shook his head. "I thought we might dance."

Her eyes widened. "Dance?"

Mitch fought a surge of frustration at her obvious dismay. Hiding his annoyance, he smiled instead, allowing just a touch of cynicism to show. "I assumed you'd heard of it, since you've spent most of the evening doing it."

He slipped an arm around her waist and lifted his free hand, palm toward her. "You hold this one."

She swallowed visibly, which didn't do a thing for his ego. Neither did the fact that she didn't place her hand in his. "I'd rather not."

"Hell," he grumbled, taking her hand and lacing their fingers together. "It's a dance, Elaine." Only two thin layers of fabric separated his hand from her skin. He spread his fingers on her back and her muscles tensed. "Part of the deal was that you and I act like friends." Her scent invaded his senses. Orange blossom? He'd never noticed how nice orange blossoms smelled until the fragrance mingled with her unique essence.

"Not all friends dance with each other."

He felt ironic laughter rumble in his chest and it surprised him. Why did her sullen comment amuse him? He should be annoyed. "You're a hard case, Mrs. Stuben."

"If that isn't an example of the pot calling the kettle black, I don't know what is!"

They moved imperceptibly to the slow, seductive melody. He held her close, his hand at her back sensitive to each subtle shift and variation in her movements. "You dance well," he murmured against her hair.

She didn't respond, merely continued to follow his lead. Though she didn't lay her head on his chest, her face was close. He could feel her warm breath through his shirt. He peered down and noticed her eyes were closed. Was she trying to block out the fact that she was in his arms?

"What are you thinking?" he asked, unable to help himself.

Her eyes opened slowly and she glanced up at him. The shock of what he saw plowed into his gut like a bulldozer. Those lovely eyes shimmered with tears. Blast! Was he so detestable she couldn't even tolerate a single dance?

"Are you sure you want to know?" she whispered.

Trying to ignore the jab of guilt, he flicked his glance

away. "It'll be over in a minute," he growled. A familiar face at the ballroom's entrance caught his attention. "Well, well…" He let the sentence drift off.

She looked up. He knew she would. "What?" From the trepidation in her eyes he also knew she knew what he was about to say.

At the sight of her face, something inside him tightened like a fist, but he squashed his compassion. This was why she was here. He inclined his head toward the front entrance. "It's showtime, princess," he warned softly. "Your father-in-law just walked in."

Dancing in Mitch's arms, Elaine's breathing came in strangled little gasps. With his distressing bulletin about her father-in-law, what little breath she'd managed to drag into her lungs froze. That's all she needed! Why did Paul have to show up? She'd almost begun to think she would make it through the whole, stressful night without another sordid blowup.

She'd also almost begun to believe she would make it through the entire evening without *this*. Her worst fear, even over and above being reamed out in public by her father-in-law, was being held in Mitch's arms.

She didn't want to dance with him. She didn't want to feel the solid heat of his body again. She had gone a little mad last night when she'd almost fallen and her scrambled brain had somehow found him irresistible— for a split second, certainly no more!

She couldn't cope with his arms around her! She couldn't cope with the troubling thrill of inhaling him. He smelled better than any bloodless beast ought to smell.

His hand at her back was gentle for a brute's hand and he danced like a dream. She hated herself for having such soft and mushy thoughts. How could she ever admit them!

What if he'd said, "Yes, Elaine, I want to know exactly what you're thinking." She'd have been in trouble. The sad truth had her near tears. Drat her stupid hide. Didn't she know better than to hand her heart to another controlling tyrant?

If there was an up side to this dance, Mitch was right when he said it would soon be over. Lucky her. Facing Paul's fury would almost be a relief.

"Okay," he whispered, his lips brushing her ear. "Let's go."

She started, the lingering warmth from the stroke of his lips tantalizing without mercy. Had the melody ended? She blinked, light-headed and confused.

Oddly dazed, she allowed him to tow her through the throng. When they emerged from the dance floor, he released her hand and slipped his arm about her waist, reminding in a whisper, "Remember, we're pals."

She nodded. "I know…" She heard the croak imitating her voice and tried again. "I know the deal." Her head pounded as she looked around, sensing Paul's presence.

Suddenly there he was. Not three feet away. Unaware of their approach, he flourished a glass of whisky and chatted with a prosperous-looking middle-aged couple. Elaine had a feeling he wasn't at his most clear-headed. Though he was dressed impeccably in a tux, his hair precisely combed, there was a gray cast to his jaw that told her he hadn't shaved. He burst out laughing, the sound more wrought-up than mirthful. The couple he was with exchanged confused glances.

Elaine's heart went out to her father-in-law. Though

he appeared essentially cultured and elegant, the five-o'clock shadow look macho and "in," she sensed in Paul's case, it was a glimpse of a man on the verge of a breakdown.

She came to an abrupt stop. "I *can't!*" Twisting out of Mitch's casual embrace, she faced him. "I won't do it!" she cried in a whisper. "It's cruel." She indicated her father-in-law, praying Mitchell Rath had the capacity for compassion. "You don't know him the way I do. He's suffering. He's fragile. Don't force this confrontation. If you just open your eyes you can see what I'm talking about. Even you can't be that hardhearted!"

Mitch's gaze burned into hers, the silence between them drawn out and heavy. His face went grim; an artery throbbed in his temple. The old cliché, *You're beautiful when you're angry* flitted through her brain. He was quite a stirring sight towering there, his gaze flashing a warning about their deal, and how her misplaced pity was about to cost her the Stuben mansion.

He opened his mouth to speak, but his gaze shot to somewhere over her shoulder.

Had Paul spotted them? She put a hand on her chest and inhaled deeply, preparing for the showdown.

"All right," Mitch muttered, surprising her by taking her hand. "He's so smashed, it'd be a waste of time."

Before Elaine knew what was happening, Mitch had led her back onto the dance floor.

"What—what are we doing?"

"What you begged me to do."

"What I…" She felt disoriented as he took her into his arms. "I never begged to dance with you!" *Not out loud, I didn't,* she cast out mentally. *Okay, maybe a*

*few, foolhardy corpuscles in a demented hunk of gray
matter begged—a little—but I never begged out loud!*

He shook his head at her, a tiny, cynical flash of
teeth showing itself in the dimness of the dance floor.
"You're a real ego boost. And trust me, I know you
never begged to dance with me. You begged me to
leave the old man alone."

"Oh..." How could the touch of his hand make her
so addled? She cast a glance beyond the dance floor
where Paul had been. He was still there, swinging his
glass around as he talked. She cast her confused glance
up at Mitch. His face was close, too close, and he gazed
down at her radiating way too much sexual magnetism.

"You took pity on him?" she asked, unbelieving.

He shook his head. "Don't say that."

"Why shouldn't I, if it's true?"

His nostrils flared. "Because I don't want it to be
true. Let's just say I had a raging need to dance."

She experienced a rush of gratitude for his act of
mercy. "You did," she insisted with a hesitant smile.
"You *did* take pity on him." She stared in amazement.
"Considering why we're here, I know it must have
taken a lot for you to sacrifice a chance like that."

Frowning, he shrugged in what looked like an un-
willing concession. "However you may feel about
what I do and why we're here, I don't take unfair advantage of people."

She looked sharply at him, but decided not to taint
the moment with an argument. "Paul's in worse shape
than I'd feared."

The music swirled around them, voluptuous and romantic. Mitch danced well, his lead easy to follow, and
she found herself relaxing in his embrace. He'd done
a charitable thing, and that fact had a softening effect

on Elaine. The warmth of his fingers spread at her back sent pleasant jolts through her, and her breasts tingled with the contact of his hard torso.

He unlaced their fingers and pressed her hand against his chest, shielding it with his own. She could feel the steady beating of his heart. That intimacy of experiencing the strong, masculine rhythm was an explosive thrill.

"Elaine," he said, his voice low, seductive.

She lifted her face to meet his gaze and was surprised to find his mouth a mere heartbeat away. "Yes?" The word was almost a sigh of longing. She didn't care to analyze for what.

He didn't reply immediately, his gaze lingering on her lips. She forgot to breathe, some unruly part of her begging to be kissed, pleading that this time he lower his mouth to hers and—and…

"I'm afraid I'm about to insult you, again," he said, "but I have to say this."

She was too aware of his scrutiny, and wished she knew what was in his mind. He'd seemed on the verge of actually kissing her, then—*now,* he warned her he was about to insult her? She tried to drag herself back to reality, vowing not to give him the satisfaction of sensing the foolish regret crushing her chest. With a counterfeit laugh, she said, "Insult away. Our relationship thrives on insults!"

He arched a skeptical eyebrow. "Right, for a minute it almost slipped my mind." He cocked his head slightly, his breath warming her cheek. "Frankly," he whispered, "the only area where you've shown bad taste is in your choice of husbands."

Stunned by his blunt declaration, she took in a quick, sharp breath. "What did you say?"

Soberly he watched her reaction, without the slightest hint of repentance. "You heard me," he said, his tone hard.

"Why—why would you say such a thing?"

"Because, I've been thinking. And I've realized it was your husband who made that hippie with bad taste remark. Didn't he?"

The mention of Guy siphoned the blood from her face. She felt cold and shivered. Mitch's gaze narrowed. Clearly he'd felt her reaction. "That's what I thought," he growled. "Not only was Guy Stuben an ass, but he was a *stupid* ass."

She opened her mouth to argue, then could find no words. To hear someone, anyone, say out loud what she knew in her heart to be true but was too ashamed to admit, was more than she could deal with, let alone respond to. She shook her head, speechless and confused. How could this man of all people, be so discerning, so acutely perceptive to the abysmal flaws of a man he'd never even met?

"He's the reason for your business failure, too."

It hadn't been a question. Mitch had stated a fact. He knew.

Experiencing a warring of emotions, deep regret and amazing gratitude, tears welled in her eyes. For so long she'd wanted somebody, *anybody,* to understand how it had really been. And now someone did. How was it possible the man she knew to be a cold-blooded blackmailer could have such sensitivity?

She blinked to staunch the threatening torrent. She would not cry! She would not melt in a pathetic puddle at his feet. "I can't talk about it," she murmured into his chest.

The orchestra moved smoothly from one soft, sensuous melody to another. A whole chorus came and went before Mitch spoke. "Then, we won't talk about it," he said gently.

The love song ebbed and flowed as she swayed in his embrace. His arms seemed so sheltering. How long had it been since she'd felt secure? And why did she feel that way now?

"Elaine, look at me," he commanded softly.

Without hesitation, she lifted her head. His hand at the small of her back, pressed her closer. The sensuous nudge of thigh against thigh seemed too suggestive for a mere dance. She found herself clinging to him, pressing eagerly into his embrace.

His breath, warm and moist against her lips, made her heart race. "Your dress is beautiful." His lips brushed hers with the feather lightness of a butterfly's wing, sending a thrill of anticipation racing along her spine. "And so are—"

"You killed my son!" The accusing snarl from directly behind her broke the spell like a bullet piercing a plate-glass window. A clammy hand clutched her wrist, swung her around, yanked forward and abruptly let her go.

Stunned by the sudden attack, Elaine had to scramble to keep from falling. "You killed him and squandered a fortune!" Paul Stuben stood before her red-faced, his teeth bared. His slurred accusation rang in a room that had gone stone-cold quiet.

"Mr. Stuben," Mitch said, "If I were you, I wouldn't—"

"This is my problem," Elaine interrupted, placing a halting hand on his arm. Though her nerves hummed like power lines, she shook her head at him. "I can handle it."

Mitch frowned at her, as if to say she should rethink her decision. She smiled wanly to reassure him, shifting her gaze to her seething father-in-law. His belligerence was so tangible, she could feel its blistering heat.

"So," Paul said with a nasty sneer, "You're already out and about flaunting a new conquest, while my only son lies in his grave!" He pointed, shoving his whiskey glass in her direction, splashing his drink on his sleeve. *"Have you no soul!"*

He circled them, pulling down on his cheek, an unsettling gesture that made him look unbalanced.

"What next, you *she-devil?*" He jabbed at her with a thin finger, the thrusting action almost a physical attack. Elaine stood her ground, unflinching, her sense of right and wrong crying out that she defend herself. But what good would it do? Paul was in no condition to listen to reason. In his drunken, despairing state, he would only believe his deluded brand of the truth.

"Go ahead, gold digger witch! What's your plan? *Tell us all!*" He made another cycle around them, his eyes savage. "Maybe the law can't touch you for killing my boy, but I won't let you forget!"

He pitched forward unsteadily, but caught himself. His boozy gaze swung from Elaine to Mitch as he gulped down his drink.

Though reluctant to argue with her father-in-law in public, Elaine couldn't let such a damning statement pass. "Paul," she said, her tone kind but firm, "I would never have wished Guy harm. You know his death was an accident—"

"Shut up!" he snapped. "You killed him as surely as if you'd pushed him off a cliff!" With a disjointed flourish he flung the crystal tumbler to the wood floor.

It shattered, shards skittering alarmingly close to her feet.

Paul's physical assault so shocked Elaine she was momentarily immobilized. She was barely aware that Mitch had stepped in front of her.

CHAPTER SEVEN

PAUL'S glass shattering so near Elaine's feet had crossed a line for Mitch. He could no longer abide by her desire to handle this alone. Furious at the man's violence, he scowled at Paul Stuben. The older man tugged at his cheek again, the bizarre mannerism fairly shouting, *Unhinged!*

Mitch's gaze snapped to Elaine, at her pallor and shock. Her obvious pain worked on him, cut at him. It was then he had stepped in front of her.

An uneasy silence hung in the air as Mitch focused on Elaine's father-in-law—a hostile, sulking drunk hauling around a millstone of rage, enough to steal his reason. His red-veined eyes flamed with vindictiveness, but Mitch could also see the shimmer of sorrow in their depths. Paul's breathing was raspy. His face blazed red; sweat beaded his forehead. He didn't look well.

Mitch found his anger abating, and felt a rush of grudging pity. Instead of the growled censure he'd formed on the tip of his tongue, he stepped forward, placing an arm about Stuben's quivering shoulders. "You're not yourself," he said quietly, steering him away from the center of attention. "You need rest. It's time to go home." He caught sight of Marlon Breen and signaled him forward.

"Who are *you* to tell me what I need?" Paul demanded.

The tottering older man didn't resist Mitch's gentle but forced march toward the ballroom's exit. He stumbled, listing into Mitch's solid strength, responding more like a drained child than a furious industrialist. "I'm not going anywhere I don't want to go!" he whined.

"Of course not." Mitch continued to guide Paul away, his tone mild and agreeable.

Breen came up to them, plainly disturbed. Mitch said, "Can you get him in a cab?"

Breen nodded. "Certainly. Thank you for what you did." He murmured something to Stuben in a kindly voice. Mitch removed his arm from about the inebriated man and Breen took over, piloting him away from the mesmerized throng.

Mitch walked quickly back to Elaine as she sparkled there, so lovely, her green eyes clouded with melancholy. The sight made him feel like he'd been gored by a bull.

The last thing Elaine Stuben wanted was to ruin the poor, despairing old patriarch. To have such cruel, baseless accusations bellowed out in the middle of a crowded dance floor before several hundred shocked witnesses—well, it wasn't anything Mitch had anticipated or wanted.

He reached her side and draped a protective arm about her. "Elaine?" he whispered, drawing her gaze. When their eyes met, Elaine's misfortune became his. This sense of connection alarmed him. After a pause during which he grappled for self-control, he murmured, "Let's go." With his hand at her back, he led her from the ballroom, still warring against stirrings of vulnerability.

Hadn't he spent his adult life avoiding emotionalism? There was no room in him for silly sentimentality. What the hell had he been thinking, whisking Paul

Stuben out of the spotlight, sending him home? What did he care if the man made a jerk out of himself? Wasn't proof of Paul's instability exactly what he needed to convince the board he was unfit?

Anger surged in him. Blast his predisposition to being a pushover. Blast his parents for passing along that weakest of all genes! He would not be affected by Elaine's beauty, her courage or her everlasting soft-heartedness. He was a man accustomed to being in charge of his emotions, not being buffeted and manipulated by them.

Just now, in the club, he'd swung from fury to compassion to dejection back to anger—an unsettling array of emotions he did *not* care to repeat.

Before he realized it, he'd retrieved Elaine's coat and was helping her into it. In silence he walked with her out into the clear, cold night. The clouds had drifted apart to reveal a full moon. The snowy landscape seemed almost as bright as day.

He started to hand the parking ticket to the valet, but Elaine touched his arm, staying the move. "Let's walk to the car," she said.

He glanced at her and saw the solemn plea in her eyes. Nodding, he slid the valet a tip. "We'll walk."

The valet smiled, pocketed the bills and backed off, content to retreat to the warmth of the foyer.

Determined to remain civil, but invulnerable, Mitch offered Elaine his arm. She was a pawn in his game, nothing more, no matter how seductively she glittered in her evening dress. No matter how ruthlessly her body beckoned beneath the gossamer gown. No matter that her eyes stirred him, her lips drove him to distraction. No matter that he had almost kissed her while they danced.

He frowned at the memory and looked away, scanning the tops of an ocean of cars. It would be best to keep his mind on the problem at hand. How to find one silver Mercedes among the many.

They walked toward the cars without speaking until Elaine broke the silence. "You puzzle me."

He glanced at her, confused. "What?"

She peered at him, her expression inquiring. "I'm beginning to wonder if you're really the heartless beast you lead people to believe."

He frowned, not liking where this was going. "I don't know what you're talking about."

She hugged his arm tighter. Had she been anybody else he might have mistaken the squeeze for actual affection. "You were kind to Paul," she said. "I thought you were going to hit him, but you were kind."

Mitch winced at hearing his lapse out loud. He didn't know how to respond. Had the feather-light brush of her lips on the dance floor made him go temporarily insane? Restless and annoyed with himself, he responded dismissively, "It won't happen again."

"You're so tough," she teased.

He cast her a dubious look. Why had the rebuke sounded like a show of regard? "What are you thinking?" The question was sharp-edged. "Don't read anything more into what I did than it deserves. I only wanted..." His justification tapered off to nothingness. *Blast it to hell, what did I want?*

"You wanted to defuse the situation," she said. "You took pity on my father-in-law. You wanted to shield both of us from further hurt and humiliation." She released his arm and clasped his hand. Coming to a halt, she effectively forced him to face her.

She shook her head at him, her expression exhibiting

a surprising lack of her usual hostility. "You did a heroic thing, especially considering why we were there. I watched you hand Paul over to Marlon. You didn't even try to make any headway with him, as far as any meeting goes."

In the bright moonlight her eyes shone, assuring him at least at this moment in time, she didn't see him as a monster. "Stuben was drunk. Tomorrow he wouldn't remember his own name let alone anything I'd say," he muttered. *Don't admire me, Elaine,* he warned with his eyes. *I'm going to disappoint you royally when this is over.*

"There is hope for you, yet, Mitchell Rath," she murmured, foolishly discounting his silent admonition.

He opened his mouth to make the warning very clear, but somehow no words came. He couldn't understand why. Was it her naked candor, the touch of her hand, her eyes, full of approval, or merely the moon-filled night? Whatever the cause, a thought— unbidden and jarring—forced its way into his mind.

Elaine Stuben needed kissing.

Was it some cosmic prank that made her cant her chin slightly upward, daring him to follow the wild notion through to its conclusion? Her eyes shone in the false light like white-gold pools of encouragement. Dazzling, mesmerizing, challenging. His gaze slid to her mouth, those luscious lips, finally lifted in a smile. Did she realize this was virtually the first moment she had smiled for him, alone?

Suddenly the internal battle he'd fought to keep his distance became too much. No longer could he staunch the electrified need raging through him. His hands slipped up her arms, drawing her closer. He only caught a flash of the awe—or was it shock—in her eyes before he gathered her into his arms, crushing her to him, claiming her lips.

When Elaine realized Mitch's intent, her pulse skittered and a delicious shudder heated her body. Her lips had been slightly open in a smile when their lips met and he kissed her, long and hard. Without allowing herself to consider the whys and wherefores, she allowed herself to become lost in the world-toppling sensations.

Though the night air was subfreezing, Mitch's kiss scorched. As he clasped her against his hard, lean heat, he was all fire, all passion. He tasted heavenly. His kiss hinted at mystic and miraculous secrets he could reveal, yet only teased her with as he sampled and provoked.

This was not the kiss of a bloodless beast. This was the kiss of a flesh-and-blood man. And not just any flesh-and-blood man, but one who rarely unleashed his passions, because when liberated, they were so intense, so staggering, regaining dominion over them would be a struggle almost beyond enduring.

This understanding put another crack in the barricade she had erected against him—against the ruthless vulture who took away the thing she'd built and loved most in the world. But he was the same man who had protected her tonight, and who had shown compassion for the very man who was his prey. Was this the behavior of a predator?

His kiss gave her a deeper, more powerful insight into the man who spent much of his life concealed behind the mask of aloofness and invulnerability. Mitchell Rath was vulnerable, tremendously so, and no stranger to wall-building himself. A shiver of wanting coursed through her, and she willingly deepened the kiss, sanctioning ready access to her inner, sensitive recesses.

His acceptance of her invitation brought on a titillating rush of feeling and she grew dizzy with longing. Erotic sensations drove her to the brink of madness. The solid, sexy feel of his arms about her, his hands gently exploring, the familiar, exciting scent of his skin and cologne, made her ache with need.

"Mitch..." she cried against his lips, an unnerved plea, for what she dared not contemplate.

At the sound of his name, he paused, hesitating in his tender ravaging of her lips. Raising his mouth a handsbreadth from hers, he stared into her eyes. Something dark flickered across his features and his mouth curved into a frown. *"Damn!"* he muttered, releasing her and stepping back.

His retreat was so unforeseen, so unwelcome, Elaine could hardly maintain her balance. His kisses had turned her body to liquid fire and she felt as insubstantial as smoke. Losing his solidness, she swayed unsteadily, all too aware smoke would have handled his withdrawal with less stumbling and tottering. *And far less regret!*

He took her arm, steadying her. "That was my fault," he said gruffly, urging her toward the parking lot. "I'm sorry. Forget it happened."

Forget it happened. Mitch's order echoed in Elaine's head all night and well into the next day. *Forget it happened.* Easier said than done. She knew that for a fact, since she'd spent too many waking hours trying with all her heart to do exactly that.

Forget it happened!

The "it" in question was far and away the most

significant thing that had happened in her life. Forgetting it happened would be one tall order. Like forgetting a beautiful melody, or how welcome the sun feels when clouds suddenly part on a chilly, autumn day.

She sat unmoving in the wide window seat in her bedroom, watching snow fall. The weather report that morning warned of a potential blizzard. She was afraid that's what Old Man Winter had on his mind as she halfheartedly watched snow swirl and leap in gusts of wind.

Against her will her glance shifted. Mitchell Rath stood about twenty yards away, using an ax to chop up a dead tree. She watched him work with what she wished was complete indifference.

Last fall, just before she'd had to let the help go, a burly gardener's assistant had cut down the dead tree. Before it could be chopped up for firewood, she'd had to dismiss the yard crew. So it had remained there, a stark memorial to the felling of her hopes and dreams.

Why Mitchell Rath had taken it upon himself to go outside and chop it up in such awful weather was beyond her. He'd been at it for hours. The pile of wood he'd created had grown into a veritable mountain. Mr. Sunny California must be missing his workouts at the gym pretty badly, if he'd decided chopping up a forty-foot tree would replace an hour on the treadmill and another one pumping iron.

Who was she to complain? It kept him out of the house and away from her. If he was true to his original deal and the mansion stayed in the Stuben family, next year her father-in-law would have enough firewood to last him through a very long, hard Chicago winter. She only hoped next year Paul Stuben would be much recovered over the irrational wreck he had been last night.

Since today was Sunday, Paul wouldn't be at work, so as far as Mitch's quest to connect with her father-in-law, today was a waste. To Elaine's mind, it was just as well. After last night, Paul would have a terrible hangover. He'd be too ill to see anyone or go anywhere. There was no chance for them to run into him, since the last place in Chicago she would be allowed entrance was her father-in-law's Lake Shore Drive penthouse.

She wished she had something to occupy her time besides watching the glacial Mr. Rath with the sinfully hot kisses swing that ax. She also wished she'd never been let in on the fact that his kisses were anything but glacial! She found herself running her fingers over her lips, recalling the sensuous feel of his mouth against hers, of his tongue—

She cringed, closing her eyes. What did she think she was doing, dwelling on the very thing he'd so harshly told her to forget? She opened her eyes to glare at him as he raised the ax above his head. With a mighty swing, he split the log, its newly created halves hopping and jouncing off the stump into the snow.

He shifted the ax to his right hand and with a quick flick of the wrist thrust it at the stump where it stuck. He gathered up an armload of fallen wood and carried it toward the house.

He wore no hat; his dark, tousled hair glistened with snow. A white frosting festooned the shoulders of his green wool work shirt. They were great, strong shoulders. She wondered if the shirt was his or if he'd found it in the gardening shed. She didn't recall any of the yard crew having shoulders like that, though she doubted Mitchell Rath had any use for wool work shirts in his job, or in temperate California, for that matter.

"Knock, knock?"

Elaine started, then realized her aunt was at the door, not the man with the hot kisses.

"Yes, Aunt Claire?" She cleared the roughness from her voice. "Come in."

The door creaked opened and her aunt pushed inside carrying a couple of thick candles in ornate holders and a heavy-duty flashlight. "Just in case we lose electricity." She deposited them on the dresser and fished in her jeans' pocket. "Mustn't forget the matches." She lay a thin matchbook beside them. "We're supposed to get a doozy of a snowstorm. Weatherman's saying two feet by morning."

Elaine made a face. "Lucky us."

"I told Mitch to haul the wood up here to your room."

Elaine experienced a twinge of anxiety and twirled around, lowering her feet to the floor. "*What?* Why?"

Claire shrugged. "Well, you've got a nice, big fireplace and we can close off this room better than the parlor or the living room. And the rest of the fireplaces have long since been closed off. If we lose electricity, it'll be easier for us to stay warm in here."

"Us?" A nervous shiver skittered along her spine. "By *us* you mean you and me, right?"

Claire sat down on the dresser stool, clamping her hands over her knees. "Yes. Us—and Mitch." She eyed her niece dubiously. "Or would you rather he cut all that wood then freeze to death for his trouble?"

Elaine slumped against the cold window. She could answer that, but she had a feeling Claire might not see the benefits of sharing the house with a six-and-a-half-foot icicle. "Please," she muttered, eyeing heaven, "let us *not* lose electricity." The last thing she wanted was to share a bedroom with this man. At least one thing about "us" worked in her favor. Her aunt would be there, too.

What are you afraid of? she asked herself. *Don't you remember what he said? Forget it happened. That pretty much says it all, Elaine. He's not looking for a rematch!* A little voice chided, *Or are you afraid you'll jump him?*

She lowered her head, blowing out her breath in frustration. "Well, if we're all going to camp out in here, tonight, maybe we'd better break out a sleeping bag for—you know who."

"Yep, I know who—*me*." Claire rubbed her arms. "If the power goes off, I'm sleeping as close to the fire as I can get. Frostbite in my toes on that hiking trip in the Rockies last March taught me a big lesson. I don't do cold."

Elaine hopped to her feet. "Great." She replied then suggested sarcastically, "Mr. Rath and I can share the bed. What a swell idea."

"If we do, Elaine," came a troubling male voice. "Maybe you should call me Mitch."

Claire laughed as he appeared in the doorway, a stack of wood in his arms. "Touché!" She gestured broadly. "Come on in. Drop that stuff in the copper bin. Lainey and I can stack some in the inner hearth so we'll be ready for the worst."

Elaine wanted to scream that nothing could be worse than being kissed erotically then commanded to forget it happened!

She watched Mitch cross the room with his burden. Melting snow on his hair and shoulders glistened, giving him a surrealistic splendor that gnawed at her. He knelt to deposit the wood, his back to her. She scanned him, his trim waist, firm hips, muscular thighs, twinkling shoulders and back. She blinked, feeling lightheaded and confused. Had the room suddenly lost oxygen?

As she tried to get her breathing back to normal, he stood and turned. For an instant his dark eyes took her in, and she became aware that even his eyelashes shimmered with melting snow. She experienced a fierce twist in her belly. His eyelashes twinkled but his eyes were cool.

His gaze shifted to her aunt. Dusting his gloved hands on his jeans, he addressed her. "I think we'd better hunker down. It looks like a bad one."

Claire nodded. "Roger. I'll get some sandwiches made." She turned to Elaine. "Give me some help, Lainey?"

Elaine glared after Mitch as he stalked across the room and disappeared, then belatedly turned to her aunt.

The older woman eyed her with an amused frown. "Well, Lainey?"

"Huh?" Elaine had lost the thread of the conversation.

"I said, 'Will you help me make some sandwiches?'" She canted her head inquisitively. "Or would you rather make a career out of watching Mitch? So far today that's all you've done."

The accusation jolted Elaine out of her demented stupor. She lifted her chin mutinously, rejecting Claire's absurd remark. Maybe she had watched Mitch—off and on. But it certainly wasn't for the reason Claire's smirk suggested. Refusing to get defensive, she turned away and stomped toward the bedroom door. ''If you're going to help with those sandwiches, Aunt Claire, come on.''

Twenty minutes later, a basket of edibles and two large thermoses of hot chocolate in tow, Claire and Elaine trudged up to her room. The sound of wood being arranged in the fireplace gave advance warning Mitch was there. Elaine girded her loins—or whatever the female equivalent was—when a person put up her guard against another person's breath-stealing sexuality.

Claire set the thermoses beside the hearth. ''Okay, I guess we're ready. Until we actually lose power, I'll be in my room sorting through some fabric pieces.''

Before Elaine even set down the basket of sandwiches, her aunt was gone. Suddenly antsy and unaccountably hot, she looked around, trying to decide where to put the food. She spied the window seat and decided that would be a good place. It would stay cooler there, even if the fire were lit. She set the basket behind the curtain. As she drew it closed she noticed the world outside had grown dark.

She sensed Mitch's eyes on her. So far she'd avoided looking in his direction, but there seemed to be no avoiding it now. She faced him. He'd changed into clean jeans and a dark turtleneck sweater. His hair glistened in the lamplight as though he'd only recently stepped from a shower. She bit her tongue, hoping the pain would block memories of the man's glorious body when she'd seen him wearing nothing but a towel.

They stared for a moment, the silence so thick a quilt made of the stuff would have kept them warm without power *or* a fire.

He stood, dusted his hands together, then fisted his

hands on his hips. He looked powerful in that stance, legs braced wide, elbows bowed outward at wide angles. Reflected light glimmered over his face, accentuating the strong, high ridges of his cheekbones, the midnight-blue of his eyes and his square jaw. The sweater showed off a well-toned torso. Despite her internal fight to ignore it, she experienced a hot and shameful joy at the sight.

"Do you want me to start it," he asked, his voice low and suggestive.

"Start what?" she demanded, wide-eyed and breathless.

His gaze narrowed as though puzzled by her frightened-doe reaction. He indicated the hearth with a nod. "The fire."

She flushed miserably. How foolish could she be? The only suggestiveness in his question had been a figment of her overwrought imagination. She shook her head. "Let's not waste it."

"Right." He pursed his lips. "I think I'll go to my room and…" He shrugged. "Read."

She nodded. "I have some—things to do." She pointed across the room at her closet, as though the things she had to do were in it. In truth, her brain was so fogged she couldn't think. "We might as well…" She hesitated, self-conscious, her mind insisting on re-running last night's debacle over and over in her head, making her unpleasantly stimulated.

"Right." He strode toward the door.

She slipped her hands in her pockets and aimed for the closet.

The room went black.

Elaine stumbled into something that hadn't been there an instant before. To keep from falling, her arms

reflexively flew around it, then realizing what—*who*—
she'd grabbed, just as reflexively let go. The very last
act she planned to perform on this earth, ever again,
was grab Mitchell Rath! Her defense mechanisms
might be sluggish, but once operational they were
fierce.

She shoved violently and heard a low grunt, but that
was the least of her worries. An instant later she landed
hard on her backside. What little air she'd had in her
lungs—due to Mitch's unhappy effect on her—rushed
out in one big blast.

"Elaine?" Mitch asked, sounding a little hoarse.

She lay flat on her back, struggling for breath, but
without much luck.

"Elaine?" he repeated, his voice nearer the ground.
"Are you okay?"

She tried to answer, but couldn't.

Suddenly, she felt herself being lifted off the floor.
In the darkness, trying to catch her breath, it was a
dizzying ride. Hating the fact that she couldn't protest,
she placed her hands against his chest. "Don't—" She
managed, though it hurt.

"Shut up," he said gruffly. "You're the most stubborn woman I've ever met!"

"Let—let me go!" she cried, the order little more
than a strained whisper.

"When I find the bed."

He smelled good. Unfortunately, all the pain-racked
inhaling she'd been doing, trying to breathe, made his
scent disturbingly noticeable as it filled her lungs and
made her go a little haywire in the head. She had to
fight a crazy need to cling to him. *Drat her stupid hide!*

"You—call *me* stubborn!" she retorted. With her
hands pressed against his chest, the fact that he felt

solid and manly didn't escape her notice. Biting her lower lip, she crossed her arms and tried to think of less inflammatory things.

"Okay, so we're both stubborn," he growled.

She felt contact with the bedspread, and as quickly as the exhilarating, troubling ride had begun it was over. "You're welcome, Elaine," he said crossly. "It was my pleasure."

The sound of his receding footsteps and the slam of her bedroom door told her he was gone.

Trying to be glad about that, she lay in the darkness, alone.

CHAPTER EIGHT

WIND howled around the house like discontented spooks. Snow hammered the windows, sounding like buckshot. The world outside seemed to be at war with the stately old mansion, trying to batter it into dust. Mitch felt akin to the abused old home as the storm bashed and pounded it from every angle. For days he'd endured an emotional beating, and it had taken its toll. He felt torn and splintered.

The fire popped, crackled, blazing its heart out. Still the drafty old mansion couldn't defeat the insidious winter storm snatching precious warmth through fissures and gaps. Mitch stood in the shadows, the encroaching chill only a small blip on his mental radar. Flickering firelight wavered and billowed over the room, revealing bits and pieces of the scene.

Claire lay before the fireplace, swaddled in an army-surplus bedroll. Only the top of her head peeped out of her khaki pod. She faced away from him, huddled toward the fire. His own bedroll lay undisturbed some distance away.

He stood, motionless, near the room's door, in comparative darkness. He had no urge to settle in. The need to sleep eluded him and he wasn't particularly cold. Perhaps keeping the fire roaring had something to do with not feeling the harsh nip in the air, but not everything.

Against his better judgment he glanced at the four-poster and Elaine's outline beneath the blankets. She hadn't moved in some time, so he assumed she must be asleep. He only wished sleep would come as easily for him as it had for the women.

He was about as far from relaxed as it was humanly possible to be, a volcano on the verge of erupting. He'd spent the day chopping the blasted tree into pieces in an effort to ease his raging tension. Ever since the dance—the kiss—he'd felt like he was about to explode.

Why did Elaine Stuben arouse him so? What was it about her that stirred to life old fears, old insecurities? He'd thought he was immune. Over the years he'd become a strong, self-possessed, even ruthless businessman. But suddenly, this past week, every time he walked into a room occupied by the redheaded spitfire, his stomach tensed and he became restless, vulnerable to feelings and urges that he feared might turn him into an illogical fool.

He'd hoped chopping all that wood might exhaust him and he'd fall into bed and a deep sleep, undisturbed by fitful, erotic dreams. But here it was—he checked the luminous dial on his watch—one-thirty in the morning. If anything, he was more agitated and hyper now than he'd been all day.

"Oh, *noodles!*"

Claire's harshly whispered complaint caught him by surprise. He shifted his gaze to her as she scrambled out of her bedroll. She sat up and rubbed at her eyes. Yawning, she pulled on her boots and tied them.

"Is something wrong?" Mitch asked softly.

"I forgot to call Ralphie Goff to confirm our dinner date for next week."

"It's a little late," Mitch said, walking over to her. He gave her a hand up. "Thanks." Draping her bedroll about her like a bulky shawl she whispered, "Oh, Ralphie'll be awake. He hates storms. He'll be too antsy to sleep." She stifled another yawn. "He'll be up reading, even if he has to light a battalion of candles. Besides, he's so sensitive. I don't want him to think I forgot."

"Want to borrow my cell phone?" He slipped it from his shirt pocket and held it out.

She grabbed the high-powered flashlight from the hearth then glanced his way, her expression contemplative. "I plan on using the phone in the kitchen, but I'll take the cell along just in case, if you don't mind. Ralphie'll want to chat a while, and I'd hate to disturb Elaine."

He handed her the phone. "Won't you be cold in the kitchen?"

"Remember, the rangetop is gas." She tucked his cell phone in her jeans' pocket. "I'll fire up the burners and be as cozy as pie." She winked. "Thanks for your concern though, sugar." She aimed her flashlight toward his bedroll. "Now get some sleep. Elaine and I are capable of feeding the fire, too. No need for you to stand guard all night."

Mitch nodded, wishing like hell he *could* sleep. "Right. I'll do that," he lied as she left and soundlessly closed the door.

He stood there for a moment, staring at the exit. He didn't want to turn around, didn't want what he knew would happen to happen. He would watch her as she slept. Watch her and—and want her. *Blast him!* If he thought he couldn't sleep before, he knew there was no chance of it now.

He heard a low, soft moan and against his will his attention darted to Elaine. He frowned, unable to keep from watching her as she moved. Her arms flailed, knocking away the blankets. Clearly disturbed by her dreams, she twisted to her side, her face coming into view. Though her back was toward the fire, his eyes were accustomed enough to the darkness so her facial features were perfectly clear. He wished they weren't.

She had a lovely, oval face and full, sensuous lips, even curved down as they were. He could detect rapid-eye movement and wondered what problems her dreams were forcing her to deal with. She was moaning long and low, as though telling someone a very emphatic "no."

Her red-gold hair gleamed and flashed in the firelight as she shook her head back and forth. Her lips opened and she mouthed something, but no sound came.

She'd worn a sweat suit to bed for added warmth, and modesty, due to the sleeping arrangements. She moaned again, and he could hear her teeth chatter. Clearly the sweat suit alone was not enough to ward off the chill.

She shuddered and hugged herself. The storm's frigid breath, wailing through chinks and crannies was swiftly robbing her of body heat.

As he observed her there, pale and vulnerable in the firelight, an oddly primitive warning whispered through him. He'd spent a good deal of his energy today staying away from Elaine, preferring to chance frostbite over being in the same room with her and that new, fool-making tenderness in her eyes. Her hatred was easier to deal with than her affection, however mild and fleeting it might be.

She shivered again. This time Mitch knew his hesitation was stupid. She was asleep and his guard was up. Annoyed with himself for wasting time worrying how this woman might somehow cripple his hard-won invulnerability, he moved to the bedside. Her scent reached up, harassing and taunting, but he kept his emotions cool and still.

Her face was ivory in the firelight. Her bright hair glowed like spun amber. Auburn lashes gleamed as they lay across her cheeks like flaming fans on porcelain. His gaze skimmed her nose, exquisitely dainty. Her chin, a little projection of stubborn determination. Her mouth, curving down at the corners, was a highly erotic pout. Did she do that on purpose just to make him crazy?

Mentally shaking himself, he banished such unwise thoughts. Leaning over the tall bed, he seized a handful of the blankets she'd thrown aside, preparing to cover her.

Before he could, her sigh stilled him. Warm breath teased his jaw. Arms encircled his neck, coaxing him close. His gaze flicked from the tossed-off blankets to her face. Her eyes remained closed, her lips parted slightly, taunting. The next instant her mouth met his in a drowsy, dreamy kiss.

He knew she was asleep, knew she was dreaming, heedless of *whom* she was kissing. He wondered who she was dreaming about and experienced a rush of envy. Unfortunately, knowing she had no idea her dream prince was *not* the man to whom she was granting her favors, didn't make her kiss any less exhilarating. His response was powerful, immediate. A hot ache burned his gut, raced through his veins, heating his blood.

Her fingers spread across his back as she pulled him down, down. Her body communicated hot, wild promises, making his breathing harsh and uneven. No matter how his rational side fought, his desire to resist slid away. Giving in to the need that had rampaged through him ever since their kiss in the moonlight, he traced the fullness of her lips with his tongue.

The kiss they shared was perfection, the stuff of legend and romantic myths, and he savored her sweetness. With a renewed intensity he took her mouth, devouring recklessly, unleashing the pent-up passion he'd held in check for so long.

A soft mewling, like the sound of a lost kitten, registered on the fringes of his consciousness. He felt feeble resistance in arms that had seconds ago clung to him. Lips that had been sweetly submissive went rigid. He heard a small gasp, felt a shove to the solar plexus, and the spell that had woven itself around his brain was broken.

With the same dizzying swiftness the kiss had begun, it ended. Mitch found himself hurled from the lofty realm of pleasure to the pit of frustration—a steep, bone-jarring slide.

Elaine woke, stunned to discover her thrilling, dark phantom was all too real. She'd dreamed of Mitch coming to her softly in the night, warming her against the winter storm and the icy wasteland that had become her life. Little did it matter that he was the man who had snatched away the last crumbs of her livelihood, or that he was a conniving blackmailer. In her dream, he came softly, a hero, her champion, his strength and his heat a haven from her frozen, empty existence. She had taken him in her arms, gladly and without restraint. Her kiss laid bare all the urgency and longing she'd so carefully walled up inside her heart.

The message in his lips sent currents of desire

through her, sizzling and soul-stirring. She could no longer sustain the complacent naiveté of the sleep state. Wakefulness intruded, disallowing her to go on evading the truth—that Mitchell Rath was really kissing her. That he was clearly willing and able to make hot, passionate love to her.

Shocked at herself for the wanton rush of expectation that surged through her, and at him for taking her as she slept, she shoved with all her strength. Affronted at his audacity and horrified at her demented, topsy-turvy dream.

"Get off me!" she demanded, breathless. "You've got some nerve!"

He was slow to back away. As he did, she thought she heard a low moan, as though the move was painful.

"What did you think you were doing—swooping down on me in my sleep?" she cried, her incredulity turning to anger.

"I thought you were cold," he said gruffly.

"Cold!" she echoed, disbelieving. "So you decided you knew just how to heat me up?"

His expression went from solemn to aggravated. "Yeah, sure." His nostrils flared. "Ravaging women is a hobby of mine." His lips twisted in a cynical smile for a split second, then disappeared; the scowl returned full-force. "It's a shame Claire had to leave. It's especially rewarding to ravage sleeping women with her closest relative in the room."

Pushing up to stand, he turned away. He walked to the fire and added a log before she could move. She glanced down at herself, noticing the thrown-back blankets. Could he have been reaching for them, planning to cover her when she'd....

She closed her eyes, praying that was not true. That

her dream had been just that. Hoping against hope that she hadn't actually reached up and—and...*grabbed him?*

She twisted around to frown at Mitch as he stoked the fire with a poker. Sparks leaped and disappeared up the flue. Flames danced and flared. His grim profile was starkly beautiful in the blazing radiance. She experienced a shudder from the embracing chill and gathered the blankets that had been tossed aside. Had she thrown them off in her fitful dreaming? Or had he thrown them aside in his lust?

She swallowed hard and closed her eyes. Mortified heat crept up her cheeks with the awful awareness that he just might have been attempting to cover her when she'd reached up and—and—

With a low groan, she hid her face behind her hands, shamed beyond words. After a minute, when she heard nothing but the assault of storm-tossed snow against the windows, she peeked out through her fingers. Mitch no longer knelt before the fire. Surreptitiously she examined the bedroom. It didn't take long to find him. He lay across the room in deep shadow, wrapped in blankets. The back of his head was all of him she could see.

She had half an urge to call out, to apologize, to explain she'd been dreaming and that the kiss she'd forced on him meant nothing. But she couldn't make a sound. Couldn't bring herself to speak. Not only because she sensed he would rather forget the incident ever happened, but because she didn't like to lie. Sadly, the kiss had meant something. Fool that she was, it had meant a great deal.

For the briefest instant when she'd awakened, before shocking reality took over, she'd felt a strange, sweet surge of being protected. It was the same feeling she'd experienced when he'd stepped in during Paul Stuben's ugly scene at the ball. Vividly, she recalled how Mitch had handled the situation, with quiet strength and chivalrous grace. That warm, fuzzy feeling—especially for this man—frightened and unsettled her. It was too intimate, too sensuous, like his kisses. Hadn't she learned her lesson with Guy—the arrogant, domineering and cruel control freak?

Mitchell Rath might arouse the odd tingle of attraction and hint of refuge, but he was a loner, a scavenger. He would fly off into the sunset the minute he got what he came after—the Stuben empire to plunder. She must not do anything foolish—like lose her heart.

Monday morning brought with it two feet of new snow and, around noon, a return of electric power. The threesome crawled out of their lukewarm shelter. Even as groggy and sleep-deprived as Elaine was, she could tell the only one of them refreshed from a good night's sleep was her aunt.

At noon Claire grated carrots for her "world famous" meatloaf. Mitch and Elaine helped, but neither spoke as they puttered around in the kitchen. They couldn't go anywhere, since the roads were hours away from being cleared enough for anything but emergency travel. And hunting down Paul Stuben, wherever he may be, was not considered an emergency, except perhaps by Mitchell Rath. Fortunately for Elaine, Mitch had no sway over the Chicago highway department. Or was that unfortunate, since he was stuck in the house with them. She sighed, realizing it made no difference as far as she was concerned. She would be forced to be with him, wherever he was.

"Who's chopping the green peppers?" Claire asked.

"They're chopped," Elaine said, holding up the plastic bowl she'd scraped them into. "And so are the onions."

"Terrific." Claire took the veggies and poured them into her hamburger mixture and kneaded them in with her hands.

Elaine reached for a potato to peel and found herself grabbing Mitch's hand as he did the same thing. "I'm peeling the potatoes," she muttered, snatching her hand from his. She didn't look up.

"If we both peel, it'll go faster."

Elaine chose not to respond. She just waited until Mitch got his potato and then reached in the bag for one of her own. They stood too near as they both peeled their potatoes, but it was stupid to grab a potato and walk to the other side of the kitchen to peel it. Elaine was an adult. She could stomach his nearness as well as he could stomach hers.

Claire formed the meat and veg in a pan, then popped it in the oven. She fiddled with the knobs. "I think I'd better get back to sorting fabric swatches for my next quilting project." She moved to the sink and washed her hands. "You two can finish up, right? Call me when lunch is ready."

Elaine watched her aunt leave with growing distress. The room was deafening in its silence. Elaine realized neither of them had resumed scraping their potatoes. She decided she'd better start. Doggedly determined to act perfectly normal, not let him know how nervous she was, Elaine turned back to her potato and scraped as though her life depended on it.

Mitch didn't. She could see his hands out of the corner of her eye. He clutched a half-peeled potato in his left hand and the peeler in his right, but his hands rested unmoving on the stainless countertop.

She readjusted her focus to take in only her own hands and the work they were doing. She tried not to detect his scent or feel his heat. Why in heaven's name could she feel his heat! She must be hallucinating that. You simply could not feel a person's heat from two feet away. She and her aunt had stood side by side countless times and she'd never, ever detected her aunt's heat!

He cleared his throat and Elaine missed the potato completely with the scraper, and fell forward catching herself on the counter when her peeler clanked to the metal surface.

"Look, Elaine," Mitch said quietly.

She knew this was coming. Ever since she'd accused him of "heating her up" last night. She knew he would have his say. She refused to allow him to humiliate her by insisting she'd been wrong to accuse him of attacking her.

"You were—"

"Just hold it," she cut in, pointing her peeler at him. "Don't even say it. I know it was my fault. I know I kissed you. Okay, I admit it. I kissed you. You did not kiss me. You didn't attack me." She slammed the peeler down, angry at herself for the lapse, even dreaming, and angry at him for making her say this. "But I didn't know what I was doing. It didn't mean anything. So whatever you might be thinking, stop it right now. Is that understood?" She lifted her chin, defiant, daring him to suggest she had the hots for him and knew exactly what she was doing, or anything else as arrogant, egotistical and insane as that.

He turned toward her, his features solemn. His silence fed her anxiety and she felt a flair of anger at herself for letting him get to her this way. She noticed lines of strain on his face, and the glimmer of disquiet in his eyes. Good Lord! Pity! He *pitied* for her and her feeble protestations. Upset, she blurted, "No—*really*—I..." She lost her voice and tried again. "Honest, Mitch—"

"I know you were dreaming, Elaine," he broke in, his voice quiet but gruff. "I know you didn't know who you were kissing. I know it didn't mean anything." He lay the potato in the bowl and put the peeler aside. "I was about to say I need to make some calls. I'm not hungry." He walked to the sink and washed his hands. When he finished, he glanced over his shoulder at her. "I was going to say you were a great help to me these past few days. I owe you some time off. We'll start again tomorrow." He dried his hands and walked out of the kitchen.

Elaine's sense of time corroded and collapsed. She had no idea how long she stood staring after him. She had no memory of eating meatloaf and mashed potatoes or of her aunt's chatter. The day dragged by with Elaine hardly aware of anything but an alien, dreary haze that encompassed her every listless, pointless move.

Mitch used his time to good advantage, talking on the phone with Marlon Breen who, in turn, made advantageous overtures to several other frightened Stuben board members. They, on their own, called Mitch, and upon hearing his takeover offer, gave their assurances they would rather bail out with something while there were still assets to bargain with than let Paul's wild eccentricities and escalating bizarreness bring on total financial disaster. All in all, this snowbound afternoon had been more successful than had he traipsed around hunting down his prey. He only had a few more board members to convince to get a majority vote.

That night, as he showered, trying to relax under the warm water washing over him, he reflected on why so often these past few days he hadn't felt clean? Was it the Chicago water? He only wished it were that simple. No. He had a bad sense it was the uncomfortable affect Elaine Stuben was having on him. She and her aunt, and their caring and forgiving way with people, reminded him of a childhood he would rather forget. Of his parents, a gentle couple, heart-on-their-sleeve types, who spent every penny they made on the sad dispossessed they had helped over the years.

When Mitch's angelic mother was diagnosed with cancer, there was no insurance and not nearly enough in their savings to either attempt a cure or even ease her pain. At the age of twelve, he swore on his mother's grave, he would not end up like his parents—poor, with nothing to show for a hard, hard life of giving but a never-ending parade of open, begging hands.

Mitch disdained the bleeding hearts of the world. To him such sloppy mawkishness was reprehensible. He knew that even today the money he sent his father went straight to the needy. The old fool. Sentimentality was an affliction of the weak. Mitch had spent his life becoming hardened. He had learned not to give in to the softer, gentler emotions that Elaine seemed bent on wringing from him.

Yet, as he connived with Stuben board members behind Paul's back, he felt a nagging culpability. Why? Even the unwelcome vulture held a necessary place in the scheme of things. This takeover bid was perfectly legal. Wasn't he doing the Stuben company and its stockholders a favor by salvaging what was left to be salvaged? With his seizure, the company would end up with a quarter of its assets rather than zero. Maybe he was a vulture, but he was also a magician who turned dross into gold. But, vulture *or* magician, either way, why feel guilty?

"Damn you, Elaine, and your wide, green eyes," he muttered beneath the warm stream. Any affection he'd seen glistening in her gaze would be swept away when she discovered he'd never had any intention of getting Paul's consent for a buyout. That he'd used her strictly to make inroads with panicky board members. "Damn you, Paul Stuben, unhinged by your grief," he ground out. "Damn both of you for making me feel your pain!"

CHAPTER NINE

CHICAGOANS, accustomed to long, harsh winters, dug out from beneath untold tons of snow and went on with their lives. And Mitch held Elaine to her reluctant servitude. On each outing constructed to see and meet with Paul Stuben, his mental deterioration was more and more pronounced. Little if any direct contact was accomplished.

Finally, the following Sunday evening, at a gala art exhibit, Mitch had contrived a covert tête-à-tête with the last needed voting board member. Toward the end of Mitch's clandestine presentation, Paul disrupted the entire event when he stumbled drunkenly into the hors d'oeuvres table and collapsed in a heap, canapés and confectionery spilling over his prostrate form in a colorful avalanche.

From the corner of the gallery where Mitch had been pitching his plan to his nervous quarry, they watched in shock as the spectacle unfolded. Paul's calamitous sprawl couldn't have come at a better time, since the decisive holdout had stood there wavering between loyalty to his rapidly deteriorating CEO and the drive for self-preservation. With Paul's collapse, the beleaguered board member shook his head and sighed, resigned to the fact that he had no choice but to agree to Mitch's terms. He shook Mitch's hand, then melted into the crowd to deal with the ramifications of his betrayal in exchange for the salvation of his pocketbook.

Mitch hated the looks he got from Stuben's reluctant defectors, but he shook off the accountability. It was their decision to make, not his. It was business, and the Stuben board knew the only way of salvaging anything was by getting out, *now*. Seeing Paul Stuben passed out under all that food was the clearest possible proof that Mitch's takeover was their best option.

He watched from the shadows, astonished to see Elaine rush to her father-in-law's side, kneeling there, unmindful of the spattered food. She wore another of her own creations, a slim silver gown. She'd told him she'd made it from old drapery fabric. On her it didn't look like old anything. As far as he was concerned, Elaine Stuben was the most spectacular work of art in the gallery.

With that pile of radiant hair, glinting in the studio's funky lighting, she was the essence of fire and ice, and every time he looked her way, the sight of her stole his breath. He knew her gown was one of a kind, sprung from imagination, hard work and talent, and it was being ruined in the crushed food. He watched, disturbed, as she cradled Paul's head in her lap and stroked his brow, headless of the damage her kindness was doing to her dress. She looked up, stricken, calling for someone to get an ambulance.

Mitch observed her, so caring, so giving of herself, undaunted by the gawking and snickering. Paul Stuben had made no secret of his hatred for her. He'd humiliated her on more than one public occasion, yet she was the only person in the room to come to his rescue. Over a hundred formally clad, glittery peers stood by, his business associates and well-heeled friends, gaping at the scene.

Mitch experienced a sudden, seething contempt for

the apathy of those standing idly by. Even as he stalked forward to join Elaine, to help her, he clenched his teeth with fury at himself for his inability to remain every bit as detached as those loitering around him. *Rath, get this grab over quickly!* he warned himself as he removed his tux jacket and covered an unconscious Paul Stuben. *You're losing your grip!*

Elaine glanced up as someone knelt beside her, stunned to realize it was Mitch. He had stripped off his jacket and covered her father-in-law. Ever since they'd walked into the art gallery she'd been fretting, watching Paul career around, drunk, belligerent and obnoxious. More than once he'd spilled his drink on guests and stumbled precariously close to fragile artwork. She had no idea what deep, dark pit of misery he was awash in, or what psychological cracks had opened up to make reasoning so skewed he didn't know what he was doing or why. Deeply anguished by his mental withering, she'd kept focused on him, fearful he was hurtling toward a fall. She hadn't realized it would be so literal.

Wiping away a tear, she smiled at Mitch. "Thank you," she whispered.

He frowned, his gaze sliding to the man. "His skin is gray," he said, gruffly. "He's not breathing well." Grasping Paul's wrist he took his pulse. "Erratic."

"Oh—dear..." Elaine looked around, upset. "Why won't somebody do something?"

"I hear sirens," Mitch said, his hard gaze on her. Elaine wondered at his anger but had no time to dwell on it. "Help's on the way."

"Thank heaven." She breathed in a sigh, laying a hand on Paul's forehead. He felt clammy. "I was afraid something like this would happen.'' She looked at Mitch. He blurred and she blinked back tears. "At least, in the hospital, he'll be forced to eat—and get some rest.''

Mitch's nostrils flared. He started to say something, but his attention shifted to somewhere behind her head. "They're here,'' he said, rising to his feet. He extended a hand. "Let's get out of their way.''

Some things were more important than Elaine's misgivings about Mitch. She accepted his hand, knowing it would be the swiftest method of getting out of the path of the emergency crew. *Besides,* a little voice in her head whispered, *he was the only person to join you at Paul's side!*

She experienced a wave of tenderness and compassion for Mitch, startling her all the way to her toes. The man who had come to Chicago to get Paul Stuben to agree to sell out to him had hardly had any chance to meet with the man, let alone convince him of the benefit of his taking over the faltering Stuben empire.

She'd grudgingly done her part, arranging these so-called "chance" meetings. Even so, Mitch's ability to convince her father-in-law of anything had been reduced to mere minutes in the presence of a man so inebriated and agitated, Mitch might as well have been trying to reason with a storm-tossed surf as it beat itself against a cliff.

She stood close beside him as the emergency medical technicians worked on Paul before quickly whisking him away.

"I'd like to go to the hospital,'' she said. "I'll take a cab.''

"I don't know why you'd want to,'' he replied. "But I'll take you.''

A warm glow of gratitude overwhelmed her and she took his hand and squeezed. The shock that flared in his eyes almost made her laugh out loud. Instead she smiled, meaning it. "You're a fraud, Mr. Rath," she whispered. "You *can* be kind. And you can be counted on—when the chips are down."

He shot her a sudden, forbidding look. "Don't confuse a lift to the hospital with character," he growled.

She shook her head at him, unable to help her continued smile. "You're so scary," she teased. Her heart lighter than it had been in a long time, she tugged on his hand. "Let's go."

After hours at the hospital waiting for test results, Elaine was finally reassured that her father-in-law would recover, at least this time. However, warnings were dire. If Paul Stuben continued on his suicidal bent, the prognosis was grim.

Exhausted but thankful Paul was getting the care he needed, unable to harm himself at least for the present, Elaine hunched at the kitchen table, picking at leftover cold fried chicken and wilted spinach salad.

She checked her watch. Two-ten in the morning. She caught movement and glanced up to see Mitch rise and refill his coffee mug. "How can you drink that stuff at this hour?" she asked with a weary smile. "You won't sleep a wink."

He had never put his tux coat back on, and he'd discarded his tie and cummerbund. The top two buttons of his crisp, knife-pleated shirt were undone, giving him a sexy, casual elegance, somehow perfect for the middle of the night. He carried his mug back to the table. "I'm immune to sleep," he murmured. His expression serious, he took his seat opposite her at the metal table.

She lay her fork aside and rested her chin on her knuckles, grinning at him. Why was it the more tormented he appeared by his acts of kindness, the more cuddly and irresistible he became? "If you're immune to sleep the same way you're immune to noble behavior, then you should sleep very well tonight."

He flicked her a dark look but didn't respond.

She watched him sip his coffee, his focus riveted on his plate. She sensed he was no more fascinated with the refrigerator pickings than she, his mind elsewhere. Why couldn't he look at her? Was he actually ashamed of giving in to his kinder, gentler self, helping the old man, accompanying her to the hospital and remaining with her? She shook her head, amazed for the thousandth time how unhappy he seemed to have her openly admire him. Why? What was it about him—or her—that made him so uneasy to know his recent acts made her feel a real and unanticipated fondness for him?

"You're a strange man," she said, drawing his narrowed gaze.

He frowned as he set his mug aside. "Don't try to analyze me," he muttered, taking up his fork. "I'm not that complicated."

"Wrong," she said softly. "You're extremely complicated. You're angry about something, so angry you fight any soft emotions you feel. That alone makes you worth figuring out. Why do you fight your gentle side? Why do you put on this hard, unfeeling front when you're not unfeeling at all?" she asked. "You feel deeply. Somewhere along the line you've been hurt so badly you can't bear being hurt that way again. So you've put on this tough-guy face. And it's fake. *All fake!*"

He lifted a forkful of salad, but with her claim that underneath the hard-hearted beast was a squishy teddy bear, he lowered the food to his plate. "You're seeing what you want to see, not who I am." Hostile eyes sniped at her. "I've warned you before. This is the last time. Don't admire me," he ground out. "You'll regret it."

It was late and she was tired, her emotions battered and buffeted for too many hours to count. Mitch's snarling didn't scare her. She was beyond intimidation. Grateful to him for his assistance and kind indulgences, and relieved her father-in-law's condition was not grave, she surrendered her defenses, freely and thoroughly.

Tonight, for some bizarre reason, the ache in her heart she'd lived with for so long vanished. She felt calm, and even with all her troubles, at peace. Most remarkably, she found herself openly admiring the man sitting across the table from her. Even as he warned her against it.

A mere two weeks ago, she'd loathed him—this man who'd taken away everything she'd worked for and loved. But not today. Today she liked him, admired him. She didn't understand him, but she knew he held within him vast, deep wells of goodness and kindness. She experienced an involuntary tremor of euphoria, all at once knowing and accepting the thing she'd been hiding, even from herself.

She was in love with Mitchell Rath.

Not the Mitchell Rath he showed the world. She loved the man he was behind the mask he wore. She knew he could be a special human being, if he let go of the fear he carried like a battering ram. She wanted to help him do that, show him kindness was not a sin to be shunned.

All of a sudden Elaine was filled with a new depth of feeling. Her heart sang as she pushed up from the table and moved with conviction and purpose to his side. Taking his face in her hands, she bent and kissed him, giving herself freely to the emotions she felt—at last, allowing the truth to climb to the forefront of her consciousness.

Yes, it was true. *She loved Mitchell Rath.* As crazy and amazing and extreme as that fact might be, it was a truth she could no longer deny. A truth she no longer needed to deny, for her heart told her he was deserving of all the love she had bottled up inside her. Mitchell Rath was not a vulture. He was a man, a human being—fallible, imperfect, vulnerable—like the rest of humanity. And like the rest of humanity, he held within him a capacity for good. Great acts of loving kindness. And to this man, this Mitchell Rath brought into the light, Elaine vowed to give her all.

Half in exhilaration and half in dread, Mitchell sensed the great significance in Elaine's kiss. In the delicacy of her touch and the tremble in her hands as she lifted his face to hers. He knew the great gift she was bestowing on him, a gift he'd never even hoped to possess. He'd spent his nights tossing and turning, trying to banish sweaty, sexy visions that wouldn't leave him alone, wouldn't give him the good grace to let him rest.

Now, here it was, his fantasy come to life, and exquisitely sweet. The earnest sensuality in her kiss was more thrilling and poignant than anything he had ever experienced in real life, or conjured in his most erotic dreams. The touch of her lips, her hands, the brush of

her breast against his shoulder, all became almost unen-
durable in their tenderness.

Blood thundered in his brain, leaped to his extrem-
ities. Though he fought it with every raging, aroused
fiber of his being, at the end, Mitch Rath's ability to
reason, his hard-fought moral struggle *not* to use her
physically, sputtered and flickered out.

Somewhere around the edges of his consciousness,
he was aware that he lifted her in his arms and, like
some plundering warrior of old, carried her up the stairs
to his bedroom. All the while he told himself she was
a bonus, an added trophy of his imminent professional
conquest.

Once cloistered inside his room, Elaine surprised
him by taking the lead. She slid off his shirt and liberated him from his trousers, unaware she was a mere
prize to him—the spoils of war. She smiled and
sweetly tantalized, beguiling as she removed her
clothes. She didn't behave like a captive, her only use-
fulness to briefly ease the lust of her conquering foe.

When she unveiled her loveliness to him he was all
pounding blood and sensitized flesh, more primitive
and feral than human. She took his hand and he followed, less conqueror than infatuated fool. She led him
into the shower, then turned on the water. It was cold
at first, the shock made him smile. She smiled back
and he could do nothing more than drink in her lovely
face. The torrent stole her curls and turned her fiery
hair dark auburn, twisting and swirling the stuff down
her shoulders and across the soft, white flesh of her
breasts.

He gasped with surprise and delight when she took
up the soap and began to stroke his chest, smoothing,
caressing, vanquishing the warrior but enlivening the

lover she intended him to be. In her eyes he could see such trust, such faith, it made him shiver with feeling, longing to be everything she thought he was. Wanting to be the man she saw, the man she was giving herself to.

He felt the eager affection radiating from her, saw the intense, silent expectation on her lovely face, pinkened in a blush. His body ached for her, ached for sexual fulfillment and release. Her willingness, their intimate closeness, was like a drug, lulling him into a state of reckless euphoria.

He pulled her to him, muttering things even he didn't understand, things about love and commitment and how he would never betray her trust, her faith. Lies, all beautiful, crazy lies, but lies he wanted to be the truth, at least for now, for the next few threads in the tapestry of eternity. He wanted to be the man he saw in her eyes. He wanted to hold her, caress her, make wild, passionate, stormy love to her, to let her know that there was no other woman on earth but her, to show her in every lusty way he knew, the solemnity and truth of that statement.

Entwined in each other's arms, he gently rocked her back and forth, experiencing an electrifying surge of excitement when she brushed a soft kiss against the thudding hollow of his throat.

Her trembling limbs clung to him, and she pressed her body into his. The sensations were so exquisite he closed his eyes, seeing stars. He couldn't breathe. He had a burning desire, an aching need for another kiss. A kiss would ease his labored breathing. This reasoning came from somewhere in the ruins of his brain. That it made no sense didn't matter.

He swooped to capture her mouth, shivering at the

sweetness of her lips. It was a kiss for a weary, frozen soul to melt into. He lingered there, in the moment, savoring her willing warmth, replenishing his life force.

Enlivened now, he showered kisses around her lips and along her jaw, grazing her earlobe. "I need to make love to you," he whispered gruffly, never telling a more agonized truth in his life.

She answered with a series of slow, tingly kisses that nearly drove him mad. "I love you, Mitch," she said, almost too softly to be heard.

Her vow, though softly spoken, came through loud and clear as she sealed it with a scorching kiss.

I love you, Mitch.

He heard the words echoing in his head and told himself that was all they were. Words. Hadn't he just whispered words with similar promises? Hadn't he been first to vow fidelity and forever? Weren't they the same lies impetuous lovers whispered all over the world, every hour of the day, to make the one-night stands palatable?

A pain squeezed his heart and the euphoric glow began to fade. Of course they were only words—to him. But to people like her, the words "I love you" were a covenant, a pledge—sacred.

A flash of savage, unreasoning grief tore through him. Thinking became jagged and painful as his brain began the excruciating process of digging out from the wreckage of his rampaging lust.

What was he doing? What had he sworn among the first minutes after meeting her, so charmingly smudged with soot at her front door? He would use Elaine to get inside Paul Stuben's rarefied society haunts. But he would not go this far! He would not take her physically. How big an ass was he now that he was on the brink of doing just that?

She had talked herself into the insane notion he was different than he was. But her self-delusion was no excuse for turning into a total, amoral bastard. *Leave her with something, Rath,* he raged, fighting his need to know her fully, to take the most precious part of her, reduce her womanly favors, her most deeply felt act of giving, to a notch on his bedpost. *After tomorrow's vote she'll know you for the double-dealing beast you are! Leave her with her self-respect!*

His belly soured with guilt, yet even so, he couldn't help placing a kiss on her shoulder. A silent, regretful goodbye.

Sliding his hands to her upper arms, he roughly pressed her away. Sick and out of kilter, his misery so acute he was racked with pain, he shouldered the shower door wide. "Go," he growled, releasing her, fearing what one more second of her touch would do to him. He might go haywire and lose his feeble grip on his good intention.

"What?" She stood there, staring, confused. The sight was impossible to deal with. Turning away, he shut off the water, taking the moment to get himself under control. He could hardly blame her for her stupefaction. He'd given her no reason to doubt the genuineness of his vows. He couldn't look at her, stark guilt cut into his soul. A soul so recently rejoicing in its apparent rebirth. In that, at least, he'd lied to himself. There was no rebirth in lies.

"I—I don't understand," she whispered, touching his hand.

With a guttural snarl he jerked away. "Tomorrow you will." He removed himself from the shower. His limbs were heavy and sluggish, but he needed space, distance from the dangerous temptation of her loveliness.

Snatching a towel off the rack, he held it out. "Cover yourself and go." He tried on a sneer of contempt, needing to drive her to a state of bitterness and hatred as quickly as possible. She would never know the act he was putting on now was the closest he would ever come to doing her a real kindness. "I said go," he repeated, his sneer a painful fraud. "Your naiveté was amusing for a while, but it's late and I have an early meeting."

When she only stood there, staring, her eyes glinting with humiliation and loss, he tossed the bath towel at her. "Get out before I teach you what happens to foolish little heart-on-her-sleeve females who try to tame the big bad wolf."

The towel fell to the shower floor. He winced. Turning away he pulled the other one from the wall rack and wrapped it about his waist. He heard a small whimper and the sound of shuffling, then the quick, light pat of wet feet exiting his bathroom.

Sickening wretchedness spread through him. He felt destitute and desolate. The look on her face, rejected and cruelly ridiculed, would ride him hard until the end of his days. Swallowing a blaspheme that stuck in his throat, he placed the flats of his hands against the chilly tile wall and slumped forward. He felt cold and slimy.

Fortunately, after tomorrow's vote, he would have what he'd come after. He would be free of this city—and one troubling pair of wide, green eyes.

CHAPTER TEN

AT TEN o'clock in the morning, bleary-eyed and exhausted from lack of sleep, Elaine peeked into the kitchen. She didn't want to see Mitch—ever again. After his rejection last night, she couldn't bear to look him in the eyes.

I love you, Mitch! She felt sick as the words came back to haunt her. He must have found her confession hilarious. She clearly had lost her mind from fatigue and stress to have made such a bizarre statement. She felt a scream of frustration at the back of her throat and she had a hard time stifling it.

What had made her blurt out such an absurd untruth? She no more loved Mitchell Rath than—than she loved losing her business! She cringed inwardly. To The Vulture. She would carry the emotional scars, deep and red, from their ill-starred relationship for a long, long time.

She still bled from the breakneck speed at which he made that I-love-you-you-bore-me reversal. He'd been whispering husky promises, vows, telling her she was everything to him, telling her the sun, moon and the stars paled when she walked in a room. Then, *blam,* he'd pushed her away—still trembling with need and luxuriating in his honey-sweet kisses—suddenly very exposed and very alone.

The world tilted and she had to clutch the doorjamb to keep from crumbling to her knees.

"Lainey?"

She blinked, sucking in a breath to steady herself. Trying to get focused, she followed the sound of her aunt's voice to the vicinity of the table. "Yes," she said, breathless, as though she'd run a marathon.

"Come on in. Why are you lurking at the door?"

Her vision cleared and she realized her aunt had a freckle-faced, redheaded guest. She took a quick, furtive survey of the kitchen, relieved to see Mitch was nowhere to be found. Forcing her legs to obey her command to keep her upright, she walked to the table and sank heavily into a chair. "Morning," she said to her aunt. Trying for pleasant, if not actually cheerful, she smiled at Harry. His cheeks bulged, stuffed with food. As she watched, he took time out from stuffing his face with pecan pancakes to gulp in a breath of air. Apparently Mitch had been up bright and early fixing breakfast. She wondered where he was, then hated herself for giving a fig.

Getting her mind on track, she grabbed the bill of Harry's cap, hovering at the back of his neck, pulled it off, repositioning it on his head with the bill forward. He hated that, or at least made a good stab at pretending to. "How's it going, buddy?" she kidded.

He made a face, twisted his ball cap so the bill was to the back and swallowed his mouthful of pancake. "Fine." He grinned, then his smile faltered. "You okay? You don't look so good."

She resisted the urge to burst into tears. "Haven't had my coffee, yet," she said, trying to sound lighthearted. "Pour me a cup, big guy?"

"Sure." He hopped up.

She sagged back in the chair, drained both mentally and physically. Thank heaven for sturdy little twelve-year-olds and the mild crushes they could feel for women old enough to be their mothers. She gave him a grateful smile as he snatched a mug from a cupboard and carefully poured the steaming brew.

"You really don't look well, Lainey." Her aunt leaned across the corner of the table and smoothed back a curl that had fallen over one eye. "Get in late?"

Claire's question contained a suspicious lilt that caused a stab of regret and pain to tear into Elaine's chest. If her aunt knew how close she was to the truth, and how wrong she was about its outcome, she would wash her own mouth out with soap.

"Here's your coffee," Harry said.

"Thanks, big guy." She gave him an appreciative peck on the cheek and took a hefty gulp of coffee. It burned all the way down.

As Harry scrambled into his chair, she glanced at her aunt. "Paul Stuben collapsed last night at the gallery. Mitch—and I went to the hospital."

"How is he?" Claire asked, her tone reserved. She made no secret about the fact she wasn't terribly fond of the man who'd caused her beloved niece so much heartache.

Elaine shook her head at the memory. "He's not well, but at least in the hospital he'll get some rest. I'm glad of that."

Claire stabbed a bite of pancake, her expression serious. "Well, I won't say I love the old rooster, but I don't wish him harm. If you're glad, I'm glad." She lifted the fork to her mouth and took the bite. While she chewed she made a motion with her fork as though she weren't quite through with her thought. When she swallowed, she added, "If you ask me, Paul Stuben is lucky you're an extraordinary, forgiving woman. Not many daughters-in-law in your situation would *speak* to him, let alone go to the hospital and worry!'' She patted Elaine's hand. ''How late did you two stay there? You look awful.''

Elaine removed her hand from her aunt's and picked up the mug, sipping to give herself time to form an answer for why she looked so drawn and haggard. The truth was out of the question—that Mitch had made wondrous, passionate love to her, said beautiful, heart-stopping things, then halted so suddenly and brutally she still reeled from it.

Setting aside her mug, Elaine shook her head, deciding to tell a small fib and save herself further discussion. ''I don't know exactly how late it was, but I didn't get much sleep.''

Claire leaned toward her niece and smiled sympathetically. ''Try not to let it worry you so much. Paul's in good hands.'' She tucked a curl behind Elaine's ear, smoothing and patting, a kind of a long-distance hug. ''It won't do to make yourself sick.''

Elaine's attempt at an answering smile failed miserably. She wished her father-in-law's condition was the only problem weighing on her mind. ''Um...'' She cleared her throat, not wanting to ask, but finding she had no choice. ''Where's Mitch?''

''Gone to a meeting.'' Claire whisked a fork full of pancake through a puddle of syrup. ''He left around nine-thirty.''

''Yeah, he invited me to breakfast.'' Harry stabbed a hapless bit of bacon. ''Ordered more groceries.'' The boy seemed to have a thought and let the fork clank to his plate. He fished in his jeans' pocket and pulled something out. ''Mr. Mitch gave me twenty whole dollars as a tip!'' He waved the bill. ''Twenty whole dollars!'' Harry's eyes shone. Elaine coerced a cheery expression, a monumental effort. That was just like Mitch. Paying other people to do his inconvenient little chores.

"He said he had a meeting with the Stuben board," Claire said, breaking through her churlish thoughts.

Elaine only half heard the words, but after a minute their meaning penetrated. "A meeting with the Stuben board?" she repeated. Confused, she glanced at her aunt.

"I think that's what he said." Claire shrugged. "I'm pretty sure. There's some batter left, Lainey. Want me to rustle you up some breakfast?"

Elaine nodded absently, a worrisome foreboding taking hold. "Why would Mitch be meeting with Paul's board? Paul's in the hospital."

"I don't know." Claire pushed up from her chair and headed for the stove. "I didn't think much about it at the time." She giggled and glanced over her shoulder. "He's so charming and funny. Seemed to be in excellent spirits." She turned away to dip batter onto the griddle. "I never thought to ask."

He's so charming and funny. Seemed to be in excellent spirits.

Claire couldn't possibly know how her portrayal of a charming, witty, Mitch, in such good spirits, stomped around on Elaine's heart. Evidently, the aborted love scene last night hadn't cost Mr. Rath any sleep. He'd been all charm and wit this morning, while she could barely sit up and talk without a concentrated effort.

She slumped forward, holding her head in her hands. Bone-weary, she rubbed her temples and sighed long and low.

"I'm sorry you're not feeling good, Miz Elaine," Harry said, drawing her sorry gaze.

She managed a weak smile, but couldn't quite lift her head from her hands. "I'm fine, really," she lied. "Just a little sleepy."

He wrinkled his nose and peered at her with concerned eyes. Elaine had a feeling he was trying to see into her head.

"By the way," she asked, her muddy brain belatedly grasping the fact that it was after ten on a school day. "Aren't you late for class?"

His scrunched face opened in a toothy grin. "Teacher's meeting day."

Elaine nodded and sat up straight, berating herself inwardly. She was wallowing in misery. Wallowing! How could she have let herself sink so low, both emotionally and physically. *For what?* Being tossed over by a manipulator and user like Mitchell Rath was no great catastrophe! If she looked at it logically, it was a blessing!

"Teacher's meeting, huh? Well, that's good news," she said with as much cheer as she could fake. Even knowing she was better off without Mitch, her misery pressed down on her like a boulder. She had the most disturbing sensation—like she was drowning, but couldn't call out for help. This foolish heartache over Mitch's scorn was something she would have to get over, all by herself. She would simply have to find the inner resources to do it.

Maybe if she kept telling herself being rejected by Mitch was not a catastrophe, one day it wouldn't be. Maybe if she told herself enough times that his lovemaking hadn't been the most sublime experience she'd ever had in a man's arms, one day it would be true.

She swallowed several times to dislodge the knot of bitter despair wedged in her throat, reminding herself to keep breathing, one breath at a time, one day at a time. She had to move on, get her mind on other things. "So—so does that mean the Star Wars marathon is on for the afternoon?" she asked. To hide her heartache, she forced a grin, feeling like a deranged hyena.

She didn't know if Harry said yes or no. Her mind was sluggish, wayward thoughts determined to make her recall, over and over, the tragic splendor of Mitch's caresses, his kisses, the hard, hot texture of his body. A wave of wretchedness the like of which she'd never before known, crashed down on her. She fought suffocating hurt, girding herself with resolve.

She vowed inwardly she would no longer play any part in Mitch's plans. She was through being his puppet. Paul Stuben was in the hospital. If Mitch wanted an audience with him, he could just slither on over during visiting hours. By now he knew she was no asset for anyone trying to cozy up to her father-in-law. Besides, Mitch would probably enjoy ambushing Paul in his hospital bed, since it would be like shooting ducks in a barrel. Or fish, or whatever you shot in barrels that was so easy it was disgusting.

Guilt squeezed her chest. Why wasn't she preparing to rush to Paul's bedside to run interference? Perhaps she would find the strength to, but not yet. She was too wounded to do much more than breathe in and out, all her remaining energy focused on *not* bursting into absurd, heartbroken sobs.

Harry's response to the Star Wars marathon, as Elaine deduced when she managed to refocus, had been no. He wanted to take advantage of the school holiday to earn as much money as he could helping deliver groceries. With Mitch's twenty dollar tip, Harry proudly announced he had *almost* enough for his new bike.

So Elaine was left without the distraction she craved. Helping her aunt sort through fabric left her mind free to wander. And as Elaine found out, a mind was a terrible thing when left free to wander! More than once she found herself gasping aloud with heated memories of her shower with Mitch.

"What is it with you, Lainey?" her aunt asked after the third or fourth gasp. "Did you forget and leave a pin stuck in your jeans after you fixed that back pocket lining?"

Elaine shook her head. "No. Just a little heartburn," she said, marveling at the irony of the statement.

"Well, take something for it. Every time you gasp, I lose count of my center squares."

"Sorry," Elaine muttered, horrified at herself. Restless, she scrambled up from the floor where she'd been hunched over a box of fabric scraps. "I'll go—take some antacid."

"Take a nap," her aunt said, frowning with concern. "I can do this. You catch up on your sleep."

Elaine nodded and brushed threads from her jeans. "I think I will." She knew she wouldn't sleep, but she hoped simply lying down with her eyes closed would help her get a little needed rest.

She exited her aunt's room, heading for her own at the end of the long hallway, when Fate dealt an ugly blow. Just as she passed the head of the staircase, something as big as a truck ascended the final step, blocking her path. She had to skid to a halt to keep from plowing right into it.

"*Oh!*" Elaine stumbled backward a step. Realization came a split second later and her heart went to her throat. It wasn't just any truck-size something, but a very specific and unwelcome male something. *Mitch Rath.* Humiliation heated her cheeks and she averted her gaze. "Excuse me," she muttered, hurrying by.

"Elaine," he called after her. "I'm leaving this afternoon."

She hadn't intended to stop, but the impact of his statement stilled her in her tracks. She turned. "You are?" *Hooray* was on the tip of her tongue, but the ache in her heart refused to set the exclamation free.

Against her will, she drank him in. Those compelling eyes, the sharp, classically handsome features, the confident set of his shoulders. His black hair gleamed in reflected light as it tapered neatly to the crisp, white collar of his dress shirt.

Standing there, exquisitely clad in a high-priced Italian navy suit and patterned power tie, he had the air of authority, the bearing of a man who demanded, and got, immediate obedience. It took all Elaine's badly corroded courage to remain there, head unbowed, defiant in her silence. "Well—*fine,*" she said at last. "Have a nice trip." She made the statement with an irascible inflection. Anyone with half a brain would know her true meaning was, *Good riddance!*

Silence reigned for several tense heartbeats before he took up the conversation. "I'm sure I will." His cool tone cut deeply. His sardonic expression sent her temper soaring. She wanted to scream and cry, and pound his chest and clutch him madly, begging for his love. What? No—no! That's not what she wanted! She loathed Mitchell Rath, with all her heart and soul.

"The house is yours."

She stared, unable to mask her astonishment.

"You did everything I asked of you."

Unhappy to be reminded, her astonishment mutated into a hostile glare. "I'm not keeping the house. It belongs in the Stuben family. I'm giving it to Paul."

He smiled blandly but his eyes remained cool. "Why doesn't that surprise me?"

She felt the sting of his sarcasm. "Financial wealth isn't the only kind. Some people achieve riches through acts of generosity—I thought for a while you understood, but—you could never understand that kind of wealth!"

His twisted grin unnerved her. "I understand it, but I don't subscribe to it. Since I know better than to argue, please accept my congratulations." The smile evaporated. "I'm sure your brand of riches will sustain you in a lifestyle of dedicated destitution."

His gibe bruised her pride. "Thank you, Mr. Rath. I hope your wealth makes you as happy as you *deserve* to be!"

Sudden anger heated his eyes, dramatic proof her verbal salvo had hit its mark.

She gave him a beat to respond. When he didn't, she forged on. "So you're leaving without the Stuben empire?" She experienced a rush of elation, heartened to discover The Vulture didn't get his prey every time he swooped!

Mitch shrugged his hands into his trouser pockets, his midnight eyes probing. "All this righteous indignation and you haven't even heard the news?"

His question caught her off guard. "What news?"

"It's been on the TV and radio."

A shiver of misgiving raced through her. "What has?"

A slight scowl touched his brow, then was gone. He studied her for a moment, his features now absolutely without expression. "This morning the Stuben board sold out to me."

Her mind refused to understand. She stammered in bewilderment, "They—they—what?"

With her tremulous question, Elaine thought she saw a spark of emotion in his eyes but all too soon they were dark and unreadable. "The Stuben board sold out to me," he repeated tonelessly. "This way they'll be left with something, not just worthless stock."

"You—you bought the Stuben empire—while Paul was in the hospital? How could that be? How could you..." Stark, bitter realization hit her between the eyes like a club. Her fury billowed and swelled until it almost choked her. "You used me—*played me,* so you could sneak behind Paul's back?" She spat out the indictment. "To—to get to his *board?*"

Her accusation hardened his features. "All true," he said without apology. "You were a great asset."

Her anger became a scalding fury, so hot and uncontrollable she rushed at him, bent on scratching his arrogant face.

He grasped her wrists, restraining her, saving her from herself. "I'm sorry, Elaine," he said quietly, gruffly. "Try to understand. It was just business."

Thwarted by crippling rage, shock and grief, she couldn't speak. Her breathing became ragged, her anger impotent. Tears of frustration stung her eyes. "You're *sorry!*" She choked out an anguished laugh. "You're so right! You *are* sorry! *You sorry bastard!*"

She jerked from his grip. "I've never heard of such a vile, underhanded trick!" She whirled away to stalk to her room, then in a white-hot spasm of fury, whirled back. "You're no vulture, Mr. Rath!" she cried, a suffocating sensation tightening her throat. The knowledge of how wrong she'd been about him last night, how she'd almost given herself completely to him, twisted inside her chest like a double-edged sword. "You're a cold-blooded, belly-crawling *snake!*" Her voice was strange to her ears, so cold, so hard. "Get out of my house. I never want to see you again!"

CHAPTER ELEVEN

MITCH'S latest acquisition, the Stuben empire of fifteen department stores, was the biggest coup of his career. Over the past two weeks he'd been front-page news across the country. In the next few months, when he sold off the Stuben assets, he would become one of the wealthiest men in America.

He shook his head, still staggered by the realization. When he'd started out, buying up defunct e-businesses, he'd had big plans, but he'd never pictured himself this wildly successful. Coming up from nothing the way he had, he'd been determined, *driven,* to become a millionaire. But now he was vastly richer than he'd ever imagined. At least, once he disposed of Paul Stuben's empire, he would be.

He drove the last mile to his dad's place, up a winding wooded Northern California road toward the cabin he remembered from his childhood. His father lived deep in the forest, his most constant companion a clear, fast-running stream a hundred feet from the back stoop. It was there, on the same flat outcropping of rock, Jeremiah Rath had caught Sunday supper for as long as Mitch could remember.

Mitch took the last bend in the rocky road, glancing at his Rolex. Nearly five o'clock. His father would be frying the bass by now. He could almost smell it cooking, hear the spatter of hot grease. He hadn't eaten fried fish since he'd left home. It reminded him too much of his poverty-stricken childhood. Even so, he found himself driving up to visit his dad this particular Sunday in mid-February. He had no idea why. He'd missed his father's birthdays before. So, why this year did he feel the need to reconnect?

The dirt driveway came into view. Mitch turned his sporty Jaguar off the gravel, slowing the car to a crawl as he maneuvered the narrow, rutted path.

The old place looked the same. Faded white clapboard, gray composition roof. Patched areas exhibited different colors of shingles, no doubt scrounged from construction site Dumpsters or donated by friends. A dented and rusty pickup truck squatted beside the house.

Mitch pulled to a stop behind the truck. He scanned the weathered porch, noticing the middle of three steps leading to the front stoop was broken. He clenched his jaws. Luckily, he'd come in jeans and a work shirt. He had a feeling he'd spend his father's birthday painting or hammering. Some things didn't change.

He opened the windows and cut the engine, the smooth, deep-throated sound of the fine-tuned motor dying. The world went still. Mitch sat motionless. After a minute he could make out the rustling of wind in the tall pines. Patches of snow lingered from the latest snowfall. He inhaled the bracing, frosty scent of winter in the high country. Memories of hard and hungry times, of his mother's illness and death, made him flinch as old, familiar discontents flooded back, full-force.

He heard a squeak and looked up sharply. Even the screen door sounded the same. Jeremiah Rath stood there, in faded denim overalls and a red, flannel shirt. The older man squinted, clearly having forgotten his glasses rode on the top of his head amid iron-gray, curly hair. Mitch surveyed his father. His features were everlastingly kind and serene, full lips blending into a strong chin. His long, narrow face was more deeply seamed than Mitch recalled. Of course it had been two years since he'd been home.

Mitch could tell when his father recognized him. His eyebrows rose in pleasure over the same midnight gaze Mitch had inherited.

He waved. "Son!" As spry as a teenager, he hustled off the porch, jumping across the broken step and hurrying toward the car. "Mitchell! You're just in time for supper!"

Mitch climbed out of his car. When his dad drew close, he permitted a hard hug, slowly encircling his father's shoulders with his arms. "Hi, Dad." He experienced a surge of melancholy emotion. "Happy birthday."

His father patted him fondly, maintaining the hug for another beat before he let go. "Birthday?" He stepped back, scratching his temple. "Is it my birthday, again?" A playful smile crinkled his eyes. "Didn't I just have one of those last year?"

"Anything's possible," Mitch kidded, trying to get into the spirit of the occasion. Breaking eye contact he bent inside the sports car and grabbed a brightly wrapped shirt box from the passenger seat. When he straightened, he nudged the door closed and handed the gift to his dad. "Lucky I dropped by or you'd have forgotten it entirely." He slung an arm about his father's shoulders, conscious of how small he seemed. Though only a couple of inches shorter than Mitch, Jeremiah was much more slender, almost bony. "So, what's for supper, Dad?" As if he didn't know.

"Some pretty fair spotted bass." He put an arm

around his son's back. "Fried onions and mashed potatoes with gravy."

Mitch could have won a million dollars betting on that menu. Sunday suppers hadn't changed in all his thirty-five years. "Are you sure you have enough for both of us?"

Jeremiah chortled. "Has there ever been a Sunday when I've caught less than five nice-size bass in that stream?"

Mitch laughed, feeling lighter-hearted. "Not in my lifetime." If there was one constant in his world, it was Jeremiah and his Sunday catch.

"The world's full of bounty, son," he said. "I'm blessed."

Mitch's good spirits flagged and he stared at his father. How could he say such a thing? Blessed? He wanted to shout, *Look at the hovel you live in, Dad! Patched and seedy! How can you call yourself blessed?* But he resisted. They'd had that same argument too many times to count.

Over the years Mitch had sent his dad more money than it would cost to buy several comfortable three-bedroom homes in some pleasant suburb in L.A. or San Francisco. But his father had frittered it all away on one charity case or another.

Not wanting to spoil their visit, Mitch held his tongue. Silently he walked up the steps with his father. They avoided the broken one and crossed the porch, its tired old planks squawking under their weight. With the accompanying squeak of the screened door, Jeremiah and Mitch entered the tiny, three-room cabin. Within seconds four tail-wagging mongrel dogs surrounded them. A handful of multicolored cats, scattered about on various pieces of worn and frayed furniture, eyed the men with little interest. After a few seconds they settled back to their grooming or napping.

"Open your present, Dad," Mitch said, absently patting one of the dogs, a collie mix with a limp. It licked his hand. Mitch was suddenly filled with a heavy, sodden dejection. So many needy beings in the world—both human and animal. Didn't his father ever feel lost, helpless, sucked dry from all the endless giving?

"Okay, son." His father lay the box on the scarred pine table next to his plate of food. "Sit yourself down while I dish you up your meal. I'll open it after we eat."

Twenty minutes later, the fried fish consumed, Mitch drank coffee from a cracked china cup. Dessert was a box of raisins set in the middle of the table. Taking a sip of the brew, Mitch inhaled its rich aroma. He'd forgotten how good his dad's coffee was. No way was it gourmet. Probably the cheapest brand available, but somehow it always tasted great.

As he sipped he scanned the box of raisins. Obviously his father remembered how much Mitch loved raisins as a kid. So had his dad. It was a luxury they'd shared when they could afford to. This box had to be a favorite treat his dad had been saving, and he'd brought it out now, just because he knew Mitch loved raisins. Touched by the simple kindness, he took a handful. That would be all he'd take, mainly to give his father the pleasure of giving the gift. He'd leave most for his dad to enjoy later.

With a contented sigh, Jeremiah sat back in his rickety ladder-back chair and lifted Mitch's gift into his lap. Carefully he began to untie the ribbons, as though he planned to save them for some future use. Mitch knew somewhere in the house his father kept a bag of ribbons from old gift packages. And another filled with carefully folded wrapping paper, ready for heaven-knew-what.

His father painstakingly opened the package, causing as little ripping of the fancy paper as he could. It was an age-old ritual that made Mitch crazy. He could buy his father all the fancy wrapping paper he could ever use!

The lame mongrel limped up to Mitch. To help keep his composure, he petted the dog. The mutt lay his head on Mitch's thigh, peering up at him with such wistful joy Mitch found himself smiling. A sweet mutt. Clearly whatever history it had, its life was profoundly better now, and it adored any small kindness, along with the human being who bestowed it.

Sitting there, his belly full of good food, in good company, a devoted dog by his side, Mitch found something unexpected—for a wispy thread of a moment—he experienced pure, simple contentment.

"Why, son!" Jeremiah pulled the green and blue plaid flannel shirt from the box. "It's perfect. Just what I needed."

Continuing to pet the dog with its poignant, worshipful eyes, Mitch transferred his smile to his father. "You're not hard to buy for," he said. "It was either a flannel shirt or a pair of overalls." He indicated a white envelope beneath the shirt. "You might find some use for that, too," he said, trying not to sound strained. The thousand dollars in that envelope would slip through his father's fingers like water through a screen. Mitch only hoped his dad would at least buy himself the basic necessities of life before squandering the rest on people hardly more needy than he.

Jeremiah picked up the envelope, hefted it and

smiled, his dark eyes aglow with gratitude. "You're a good son." He lay the envelope on the table alongside the box of raisins. "This will do so much good."

Mitch swallowed, tasting ashes. His father already had plans for the money that had nothing to do with keeping his own bony carcass fed. He counted to ten before he could trust himself to reply. "Sure—I'm sure," he muttered, with a helpless wave of his hand. "Dad…" He took a long, calming breath, deciding to forget it. He didn't want to argue. Changing directions, he finished, "Before it gets too dark, why don't you let me fix that front step?"

Jeremiah set the gift box on the table and carefully lay the shirt in it. With as much care as if it were gold, he settled the ribbons and folded wrapping paper on top. "Now, Mitchell," he said, "you didn't come all this way to work."

"I want to," Mitch insisted, standing, deciding it would be best for him to take out his frustrations on the blasted step. "You have some wood around back, don't you?"

"Well, I suppose. There's usually some."

"I have tools in the trunk of my car."

Jeremiah stood, dusting his hands on his overalls. "It's kind of you, son." He circled the table and patted Mitch's shoulder. "Really kind."

Mitch didn't respond. He always suffered from mixed emotions when he visited his father. The cabin was shoddy, but on his infrequent visits, he'd found it surprisingly restful, where the stresses of his high-pressure world faded away. And though he could relax for a time, anger at his father's reckless, openhanded spending simmered below the surface.

Jeremiah was so good-hearted, arguing with him

seemed as mean as yelling at a four-year-old for spilling milk while he was pouring you a glass. Over the years, Mitch had shouted and pleaded and wheedled, even used psychology on his dad, trying to get him to listen to reason.

He might as well face the fact all he could do was attempt to keep him from starving to death by giving absolutely everything he had to others. Lately, he'd been neglectful of his dad's well-being, building his business with a vengeance. His father would never mention it, never even think such a thing, but Mitch felt the sting of guilt.

Odd, now that he was immensely successful, his life wasn't as perfect as he'd believed it would be. He couldn't understand why. He should be one of the happiest men in the country now that he was among the richest.

For years he'd lived for the next "when"—"*When* I make my first million, I'll be happy." He'd done that several years ago, but he hadn't been happy. There had always been another "when" to conquer. "*When* I make my fifth million!" "*When* I make my tenth!" "Whens" had come and gone. Strangely, none making him the happy man he'd expected them to. Even this last "when"—"*When* I get the Stuben empire"—had been surprisingly unsatisfying.

Ever since he'd left Chicago with the biggest coup d'état of his life, he'd been short-tempered and moody. A far cry from the fulfilled conqueror he assumed he'd be.

As he repaired his father's front step, his thoughts ran on their own to Elaine Stuben, and that last afternoon. He couldn't seem to shed the bone-deep melancholy that rode him day and night. He couldn't stop playing over and over in his mind the instant those wide, green eyes filled with realization—and stark horror—at what he'd done.

He'd been forced to watch the scene over and over in his head, immobilized, seeing her lovely eyes shimmer with raw disappointment. Since that moment, a bleak shadow had taken up residence in his heart.

Damnation. Hadn't he told her not to analyze him, not to hold him in any esteem! Whose fault was it she was disappointed in the end? Not his! He'd come to do a job and he'd done it. She was paid for services rendered—a two-million-dollar mansion! That sort of fee was nothing to be sneezed at.

He banged away on the step, hoping the nails he drove into the weathered plank would help relieve his gnawing frustration.

His gut twisted fiercely as he recalled her choked, desperate laugh, her wretched expression. What was it about this woman's naive disillusionment, her soppy anguish at his deception, that could cheat him out of his victory celebration? Any problems she had with him were of her own making, self-delusions he couldn't be held responsible for. He'd warned her!

A sudden, exploding pain told him he'd lost his focus and smashed the hammer down on his thumb. He mouthed a guttural oath and dropped the hammer. "Damn you, Rath!" he grumbled. "Your preoccupation with her is going to kill you!"

"What happened?"

Mitch squinted in pain as the screen door opened. Jeremiah stepped out onto the porch wearing the new flannel shirt. Slipping his glasses down on his thin, straight nose, he watched Mitch as he shook the injured hand and muttered a string of self-directed curses. "Hit my thumb," he gritted out.

"Dang shame." Jeremiah motioned him inside. "Let's put some ice on it."

Once again Mitch sat at the scarred table, his thumb wrapped in a faded blue bandanna filled with ice chips. He set his elbow on the pine surface, elevating his hand to help ease the throbbing.

After pouring fresh cups of steaming coffee and shoving the raisin box at Mitch, his father sat down across the corner from him. Lounging back, he quietly observed his son, his expression somehow pitying. Mitch had the ridiculous feeling the pity wasn't about the smashed thumb, and grew restless.

"You look tired, son."

Mitch winced. He didn't like the direction this conversation was taking. "I'm fine," he said, deciding to make quick work of the subject. "I'm doing very well, in fact."

Jeremiah crossed his arms over his thin belly. "I heard. Congratulations on your latest business deal."

The comment confounded Mitch. "How did you know?"

Jeremiah smiled. "I have friends. They keep me posted."

Mitch should have realized. Jeremiah was rich in one regard. He had a lot of friends. "Well, then you know I'm doing fine."

Jeremiah watched his son, those dark eyes ironically compassionate, considering their very different stations in life. Jeremiah lived alone in the woods, a do-gooder who took in broken and abused animals and strangers, giving everything he had, with nothing to show for his generosity but a leaky roof and empty pockets—and *some* friends, he admitted grudgingly.

And what of Mitch? To put it vulgarly, he was rolling in money. People cowered and kowtowed when he entered a room. He had extraordinary business savvy and that translated into great power. He was respected and feared in all quarters of the nation. He had friends. Maybe, he amended, he wouldn't have quite so many friends if he were poor. When you had power and money it was hard to tell who your real friends were.

He exhaled, glancing away. An uneven tap-ti-tap drew his attention and he spied the limping mutt approaching. The collie mix laid its head on Mitch's leg. Those hopeful eyes looked up into his face. Clearly the dog didn't understand Mitch was not in the mood to comfort. Still, instinctively, his hand went out and he began to pet the pooch, his reward a renewed flare of adoration in its eyes. Mitch shook his head, almost able to smile.

"So you're going to take the Stuben stores apart, sell off the pieces?"

Mitch nodded, continuing to pet the dog, mesmerized by its eyes. The mutt didn't care how many millions Mitch had. He adored him, simply and sincerely because of a kindness. How long had it been since he'd seen that look in any human's—

A sharp slap of memory halted him mid-thought. One person had looked at him that way. For a little while, at least. Elaine Stuben never cared how much money he had. For a time during their brief, stormy relationship, she'd thought him kind. She'd looked at him with such simple, honest caring, it frightened him. And now, he was left with only the memory of her shimmering eyes, her raw disappointment and a silent, stinging sadness.

"People tell me it'll make you a very rich man."

Mitch experienced a bizarre stab, flashing his gaze to his father. Why in Hades did he feel guilty about that? "Yeah," he finally said, his lack of enthusiasm hard to mask.

His father eyed him without speaking for a few more seconds, then lifted his glasses to the top of his head. "So—you came here to ask me why you're not happy."

Mitch was too startled by the statement to offer any objection. He could only stare. He'd never heard a more absurd thing in his life.

Jeremiah smiled sympathetically. "Since you've come so far for my opinion, I'll tell you, son." He sat forward, placing his forearms on the table. Observing Mitch with gentle eyes, he laced his fingers. "It's pretty simple."

Jumbled feeling ricocheted through Mitch and he tried to force his emotions into some semblance of order. Tried to form the appropriate retort—that he was there for no other reason than to wish his father a happy birthday. To his great annoyance and surprise, the words didn't come. *Why the hell not?* With the snap of his fingers Mitch could make any number of arrogant, self-important stuffed shirts grovel and cringe. So why was it that under his father's gentle scrutiny, he was the one wincing?

He pursed his lips in aggravation. He wasn't a twelve-year-old being reprimanded. He was a powerful man! A mover and shaker! Impatient with himself and his momentary lapse into vulnerability, he insisted,

"Don't be ridiculous, Dad! I'm as happy as the next man."

Jeremiah nodded sagely, not put off by his son's curtness. "As happy as the next *unhappy* man."

Mitch frowned. Another *Don't be ridiculous!* jumped to the tip of his tongue, but his father held up a halting hand. Ironically, the gesture, coupled with the patient understanding in his father's gaze, had the capacity to suspend Mitch's argument.

"Son, you've been a prosperous man for years, now. You've had time to find out how much happiness can be squeezed out of a dollar."

Mitch's gut clenched, all the "whens" of his driven existence rushing back. He'd made a pile of money, but hadn't been able to squeeze much true happiness out of it. He glared at his father, but didn't respond. For once, he found himself inclined to listen.

"Your life is centered around tearing down," Jeremiah quietly explained. "Mine, and your mother's, has always been centered around helping, building up." He reached out, affectionately squeezing Mitch's upraised forearm. "Why not try building up?"

Mitch snorted derisively, incredulous and a little sad. For some reason he'd half believed his dad had the magic answer. He shook his head at his childish wishful thinking. His gaze shifted to the dog. He watched its eyes as he stroked its back. "What's his name, Dad?"

"Don't know, son. He wandered up here a couple of weeks ago in pretty bad shape. Haven't got around to naming him."

Mitch looked at his father. "Don't you ever get lonely, Dad?" He was shocked to hear the question come out of his mouth. Wondered where it had come from.

Jeremiah took a sip of his coffee. "No, son. I have friends and good works." Smiling, he inclined his head toward the picture of Mitch's mother, simply framed and hung on the faded, sunflower wallpaper. "And I have lots of good memories." Resettling his cup in the mismatched saucer, he leaned forward, placing his forearms on the table. "I think you've finally learned something about happiness—and the things it doesn't come from. Real happiness comes when you build something worthwhile, son. And having somebody you love to help you build it." He gave Mitch a penetrating look. "I was lucky enough to find your mama."

Casting his gaze at his mother's picture, he said, "There aren't many like her."

"There are some," Jeremiah responded softly. "When you meet your special woman, you'll know it in your heart."

A prowling unease crawled down Mitch's spine. *Not in this lifetime,* he countered inwardly. He wouldn't go gooey and soft for anyone. Vulnerability was a weakness and he'd disciplined himself against weakness. In business, in private, in every aspect of his life!

"Hmm."

Jeremiah surveyed his son's face, his slyly discerning utterance grating on Mitch's nerves. Restless, and needing activity, he stood and paced to the front window, glaring out but seeing nothing.

"I see," Jeremiah said.

Mitch didn't turn around, didn't leap to his father's bait. At least not for a count of ten. "Okay, okay…"

Mitch finally said, highly annoyed with himself for needing to know. "What do you *think* you see?"

"You're unhappy, son—because you found her, and you let her go."

CHAPTER TWELVE

ELAINE never expected to be living in the Stuben mansion after the first day of February. Now, a month later, she still resided within its stately walls. With Paul's ouster as Stuben CEO, he was ejected from his penthouse in the Stuben headquarters. After leaving the hospital, still a sick man, Paul had nowhere to go. Elaine was grateful she'd managed to save the mansion for him and had his things moved in. Much to Claire's exasperation, Elaine stayed on to care for him.

Though Paul continued to snarl like a wounded dog, Elaine knew his hostility was a by-product of his grief. With time, he would come to terms with his son's death. He no longer drank, and he was eating better. Lately, she'd sensed some softening in his manner, a renewed interest in life. She didn't think these positive changes were solely due to the easing of the harsh winter weather. She felt he would recover fully—*if* he could find absorbing work.

The second day of March dawned sunny and mild. After taking Paul his lunch tray, Elaine decided to go outside. She strolled over the lawn, enjoying the sunshine, a golden-bright promise for the return of a green and flowering world.

Though she tried to open herself to the awakening of spring, her smile was short-lived and lukewarm. She only wished her heart could make such uplifting promises—for a rebirth of hope and joy in her soul. She closed her eyes, miserable. Ever since she'd endured the horrible rip in the fabric of her faith in Mitchell Rath—the man she'd so irrationally fallen in love with—a bitter despair had shrouded her.

She'd managed to convince herself she hadn't really fallen for Mitch—for a time. She even persuaded herself to believe she loathed him. That had been the one bonding element between her and Paul since his ejection from his penthouse. He hated the man with a venomous passion. At least they'd had their hatred of The Vulture to share.

For a time.

Elaine knew any wise woman would nurture that hatred until the end of her days. Any wise woman. Sadly, she'd come to discover herself unwise—unable to keep her hatred alive.

Mitch intruded at every turn with such powerful memories they had the ability to drive her to tears. She detected his scent on her evening cloak, and at disconcerting moments, even in her bedroom.

The recollection of how protected she'd felt on his arm, the sense that he'd respected her wishes, even on small details, gnawed at her. Things like allowing her to choose a restaurant and order her own dinner. Not being involved in which dress she wore. Finding no fault with her hairstyle or her choice of fingernail polish. Letting her decide when to leave a party. All these things, large and small, Guy had been fanatical about controlling.

Heated memories of his kisses plagued her night and day. Even her dreams tormented her with hopeless, foolish yearnings. She missed so much about the Mitchell Rath she'd come to know, when they had been alone and he had been considerate, even giving. The pecan pancakes he'd made for their breakfasts. The embarrassing light bulb encounter. The firewood he'd cut in subfreezing weather. The groceries he'd bought and paid for, more than any one man could eat. Even the pizza he'd let her buy that first night. The man who had done all those kind things was the man she'd grown to—to...

She couldn't bring herself to say the word. It made her heart ache too much. Besides, such a conniving, self-serving man who would lie to her and casually use her didn't deserve her love.

New anguish seared her heart and she sank to the ground. The grass was still winter-brown, but the sunshine was cheerful, the only cheerful thing in her reality. She lay back on the grass and closed her eyes, trying to fly away in her head to someplace where Mitchell Rath couldn't follow. "But where?" she whispered to the air and the feathery clouds scudding by, too wispy and insubstantial to block the sun's restorative rays. "Where can I go to get away from him?"

She didn't know how long she lay there. She didn't think she'd fallen asleep, but something soppy sliding across her cheek roused her from her numb trance. Her eyes popped open. "What..." Panicked by the shaggy beast looming over her, she pushed up and shied away.

A furry dog stood there, its long pink tongue lolling out of what appeared to be a smiling mouth. She realized it meant no harm, so she relaxed back on one elbow. "What in the world?" she wondered aloud, running the back of her hand across her wet cheek. "Where did you come from, big fella?"

She noticed the dog wore a leather collar. Assuming it had gotten out of its yard, she sat up and fished around in the splotchy white and tan fur to see if there was a tag. She found several. "I see you've had your rabies shot. That's a load off." She smiled at the mutt as it settled down on its haunches. "Here's one that looks promising." She separated the yellow plastic disk from the metallic tags. "I'm Happy," she read aloud. A hitch in her heart made her lose her breath and she glanced at the mutt's face. "Is that your name or your mood?"

The mutt merely grinned. For some reason she couldn't help but smile back, however ruefully. "I have to admit, the name suits you. You look happy." She sighed, envying the simple creature's apparent contentment. "We'd better get you back home, Happy."

Retrieving the yellow disk, she flipped it over. "I belong to Mitch—" She couldn't believe what she was seeing, couldn't even say the name out loud.

I belong to Mitchell Rath?

She rubbed her eyes, trying again. It did say Mitchell Rath! She glared into the dog's serene eyes, demanding, "Is this some kind of mean joke?" The dog apparently didn't have any answers. It merely sat there, tongue lolling out one side of its smile.

"I didn't intend for it to be," came a masculine voice.

Elaine jerked toward the sound in time to see a male figure appearing over a rise. She stared, unbelieving, as he came into view. Tall, imposing, dressed in tan trousers and a clingy navy polo shirt that all too clearly showed off a marvelous upper torso, he kept coming.

Breathtaking and surreal, he came, so much like too many of her troubling dreams—Mitchell Rath drifting over the hill, placidly moving in her direction. Except this wasn't a dream, was it? She shook her head to clear her brain. She peered toward the low hill again, more than a little shocked to discover him still there. Still coming.

He looked more stunning and virile than ever. How could that be? How could her dreams have been so bland and pale compared to the real thing? His handsome features, highlighted by sunshine, were arousing in their masculine beauty. He wasn't quite smiling, but his eyes seemed to be lit by a flame. The sight was striking, so different from the coolness his gaze often exhibited. Her breath caught in her lungs.

When he drew near, he knelt, placing a hand on the mongrel's back. His lips curved in a flashing grin that left her light-headed. "I see you found my dog." He stroked the animal's fur.

Elaine noticed the small, caring move and her heart tripped over itself. He had wonderful hands—so able to excite and stimulate. Watching him pet the dog conjured up memories that caused pain. She hurriedly lifted her attention to his face. "Your—your dog?" she asked, weakly. "I didn't know you had a dog." The remark was lame, but she didn't know what else to say. He'd caught her so off guard, so unprepared. What was he doing here?

"I haven't had him long." Indicating the lawn with a broad wave, he asked, "May I join you?"

Not quite understanding, she nodded dumbly.

He took a seat next to her on the grass. The dog lay down and crossed his front paws. Lowering its head to Mitch's thigh, the mutt looked up at its master with worshipful eyes. Mitch lay his hand on the dog's neck, his attention on Elaine. His smile heated her blood. "Happy was one of several dogs my dad had rescued. When I visited, we—sort of—bonded."

Elaine couldn't believe her eyes. Mitchell Rath with a pet? Absurd. Especially not a mongrel. Named *Happy* of all things! She'd assumed if he ever got a dog it would be because he'd bought out some poor guy's business, and part of the spoils was a pampered pet. Elaine wouldn't have put it past Mitch to take some-body's cherished, purebreed champion, as long as he could make a buck from it. Though undeniably cute, the mutt was clearly no cash cow.

Even working at being antagonistic, Elaine trembled with the thrill of seeing him again, of basking in the stirring warmth of his smile. She berated herself, re-minding inwardly that her foolish, longing heart should know by now *not* to think of him as the man she wanted him to be.

Loathe him! she commanded silently. *Remember the man he is—a double-dealing snake!*

She lurched up to stand, taking a defensive step backward. She must not be his fool again, must not allow herself to be dragged into some lovesick stupor by his smile or his midnight eyes! He was *The Vulture,* for heaven's sake!

She steeled herself to do what she had to do, shout-ing, "I want you off my property!" She shot a shaky hand toward the gated entry. "Don't—don't make me call the police!"

If she had expected his immediate obedience, she had underestimated him, or overestimated herself. The undeniable and dreadful fact was that he didn't make the cowed exit she demanded of him. He didn't even rise. His smile gone, brow knit, he watched her, his expression pensive.

She drew an uneven breath, unsure of what to do

next. She'd threatened to get the police. Was he calling her bluff?

His features became more intense, somehow poignant. He held her gaze captive, forcing her to stare into his dazzling eyes. "I mean it—Mitch," she bluffed again, her voice weaker, more tremulous. "If you don't leave immediately, I'll call the police to—to drag you off."

In a long, tense stillness, they exchanged stares. Hers angry. His contemplative. Elaine's heart hammered her ribcage. When she didn't think she could take the punishment any longer, that her ribs would crumble or her heart explode, he finally nodded. "All right, Elaine. I'll go."

When he stood, she staggered another protective step away.

"If that's what you want." His voice and expression were the epitome of politeness, maddeningly so. She couldn't fathom why his respectful capitulation disappointed her. Did she want him to argue, to demand to be allowed to stay? Why, for heaven's sake? For what reason on earth would she want that?

You know, an inner voice jeered. *You know exactly why.*

Heartsick, hating herself for her foolish craving, she nodded curtly. In a quick spin she presented her back to him. "Then *go!*" Her plan, if you could call the muddy plodding going on inside her head a plan, was to stride casually away, showing him how dead and gone he was to her. With each faltering step, she warned herself not to faint. *Be strong,* she warned. *Don't falter! Walk away with dignity!*

"I love you, Elaine."

His declaration didn't register at first. But after several steps, each progressively weaker and more wobbly than the last, his voice nudged again, like a caress. "I do, Elaine. More than life. I know I've been a bastard. I don't deserve you. But this time I've come to you with nothing but the truth, my heart—and hope."

Her body quickened. What had he said? Confused, she twisted around, furious with herself for being such a simple pawn. Yet something deep inside told her she would be a fool not to try to decipher his quiet disclosure. It had sounded so much like... "You love me?" she asked, her tone low and suspicious.

He didn't answer right away, but after a beat he smiled wryly. "I wish you wouldn't make it sound like a threat."

He walked to her and took her trembling hands in his. His fingers were warm, like the sun, and his smile. His touch, firm, steady and reassuring, made her heart swell with a feeling she'd thought long dead, but she didn't dare dream...

"When I left Chicago I'd made the biggest deal of my career—probably of my life," he murmured. His touch was so resolute, his eyes so earnest, her defenses began to subside. She tried to restore them, but they tumbled, crumbled. His show of vulnerability touched her, resonated within her, echoing her own.

"I took no joy in my success," he went on. "I visited my dad and we had a talk. He made me see my life has been tearing down, breaking up, extracting bits and pieces from the whole to fatten my bank account," he said softly. "My parents' pockets were never full, their bank accounts never fat, but their souls were well-nourished." Mitch smiled at her with his eyes as well as his lips. "They were wealthy with hope and joy. Rich—inside."

Drawing Elaine into his embrace, he whispered against her hair, "That's how I want to be rich, darling. I thought my parents were weak, I fought that weakness. Now I understand they knew what real strength was."

He paused, holding her. She could feel the strong beating of his heart and looked up at his face, into his eyes. They shone with purpose and what she could only describe as a new serenity, a profound peace.

There could be no doubt of it. Mitchell Rath had finally embraced the man he was behind the mask he had worn for so long. Her heart soared with that knowledge and tears of joy welled in her eyes.

"I've come begging." His fingers spread across her back, holding her against him. "For your help, and Paul's. I want to reopen Stuben's stores. Rebuild them to their former glory." His smile was dear. "I see a line of dresses—your design. And Paul, when he's better, my corporate right hand. Together we can make Stuben's the bastion of quality and good taste it was." Brushing her brow with a kiss, he whispered, "I want to build up, Elaine. Not tear down."

A tear slid along her cheek as he cuddled her against him.

"Forgive a fool for being too blind to see what he needed most in life." His lips caressed her temple, sending delightful shivers along her spine. She blinked to clear her vision, marveling at the metamorphosis in his eyes, the warm hue of a summer sky.

"Elaine?" he urged after a pause. "I need to see you smile at me." His expression had grown serious, apprehensive. "I need to know you'll share my life." He kissed the tip of her upturned nose. "It's not only the business I want to build, darling. I want to build a family, have a home—filled with sweet, green-eyed little girls.''

Overwhelmed by the tender vow, she could only stare.

"I don't know when I fell in love with you," he murmured. "One day I turned around and you were there, and I was lost. I fought it, had no intention of being vulnerable to another human being. I tried to escape the truth and I was cruel, deceitful, everything you called me and more. But if you can find it in your heart to give me a second chance—"

She placed a hand over his lips, halting his entreaty, fully aware that The Vulture no longer resided in him. His brows dipped and she sensed his disquiet.

To reassure him she laced her arms about his neck and drew his face to hers. "I'm a sucker for a man with warm eyes," she murmured against his lips.

He looked charmingly befuddled.

With a low, fervent laugh, she said, "I loved you when I didn't want to. There's no turning back now."

His features lit with a breath-stealing smile. He tugged her close, taking her lips gently, possessively. Her body sang, sizzled, glowed. She sensed, at long last, she was finally home. And so was he.

Several divine kisses later, as he explored a sensitive spot below her ear, she whispered, "I can think of nothing I'd rather do than build a family with you, my love—full of green-eyed little girls." She giggled as his tongue teased and tantalized. "Maybe even a blue-eyed boy or two."

A bark issued up from somewhere around knee level. Mitch chuckled, and Elaine reveled in the feel of it. "Okay, Happy," he said against Elaine's throat. "Our children's pets will all have your stamp of approval."

Elaine's heart overflowed with unrestrained joy as she held him close. Feeling his laughter all the way to her core was an utterly sensual experience. One she would contentedly indulge in for years and years.

Their promises sealed with the kisses they shared, the Stuben empire was assured for generations to come—an empire that came to be known as "a bastion of quality, good taste, and a giving heart."

COMING NEXT MONTH...

An exciting way to **save** on the purchase of Harlequin Romance® books!

Details to follow in July and August Harlequin Romance books.

DON'T MISS IT!

Harlequin Presents®
and
Harlequin Romance®
have come together to celebrate a year of royalty

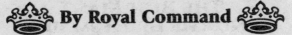 **By Royal Command**

EMOTIONALLY EXHILARATING!

Coming in June 2002
His Majesty's Marriage, #3703
Two original short stories by **Lucy Gordan** and **Rebecca Winters**

On-sale July 2002
The Prince's Proposal, #3709
by **Sophie Weston**

Seduction and Passion Guaranteed!

Coming in August 2002
Society Weddings, #2268
Two original short stories by **Sharon Kendrick** and **Kate Walker**

On-sale September 2002
The Prince's Pleasure, #2274
by **Robyn Donald**

**Escape into the exclusive world of royalty with
our royally themed books**

Available wherever Harlequin books are sold.

Makes any time special ®